CHANGING TIDE

CHANGING TIDE

ROBERT JONCAS

Changing Tide

For information about this title or to order other books and/or electronic media, contact the publisher:

Cougar Productions LLC
www.cougarproductions.com
cougarproductions@aol.com

ISBNs:
979-8-9871501-0-8 (softcover)
979-8-9871501-1-5 (eBook)

Printed in the United States of America

Cover design by: Barbara Sherman
Interior design: 1106 Design

For Loretta . . .

You always believed that you could, so you did.

*Your inspiration encouraged me to take risks
and follow my dreams.*

Jason . . .

*Your excellence in achieving your goals and your caring ways,
made me proud of you, son.*

I love you . . . Dad

CONTENTS

ACKNOWLEDGMENTS

Thank you to all my friends who supported and cheered me on while writing this novel. Thanks to the professionals at 1106 Design—Michele, Ronda, Kathryn, and Anita for your expertise and knowledge in helping me make this novel a reality.

Thank you, Barbara, for your magnificent cover design.

Thank you, Lynn, for being the best author, teacher, and mentor ever.

Thanks to my friend, Loretta—you kept me believing I could write this book. I only wish you were still here to see it completed.

FIRST CONTACT

I never thought anyone close to me would die. I know it seems unrealistic because, sooner or later, we all die. But dying is supposed to happen in the future, like getting old. When you're eighteen, you shouldn't have to think about death. The idea of death takes you to a dark place where no one young ever wants to be.

It was the second week of June, and the first faint evidence of dawn trickled into the room. I pulled the curtain back, and fog blanketed the beach, darkening my mood. But then, a peculiar light shone from the shoreline in the distance, casting an eerie glow, like a beacon, in the mist.

I pulled a pink tee shirt from the closet and grabbed a pair of shorts from the pine dresser. Finally, I jerked a purple hoodie over my head, slipped on my flip-flops, and ran outside.

The strange light in the distance glowed like a full moon on a cloudy night. I crossed the beach and drifted in that direction. The long lines of white waves that swept across the shore glowed with a warm, radiant light. I kicked off my sandals at the shoreline, treading barefoot in the cold surf. Shivering, I clutched the sweatshirt tight around my neck. The ocean swirled around my ankles. I felt tiny shells and bits of seaweed in the ribbed sand under my feet.

Last week, after my high school graduation, Mom and I flew from Phoenix to Nana's house in Crescent Cove, a small tourist town on the California coast. It was a two-hour flight from Phoenix to Sacramento, then another forty-five minutes in a small plane to the nearest airport. It would have been almost ten hours in the car had we driven. Unfortunately, Mom was in no condition to help me drive, so Nana said she would pick us up at the airport.

By the time we picked up our luggage, Nana was waiting outside the terminal in her old VW van. The trip was hard on Mom. Dark circles of exhaustion were under her eyes, and her hair hung in matted strings against her pale cheeks. She collapsed into the front seat while Nana helped me load the baggage into the back of the van.

When we drove up to the house, I knew it right away, even though it had been five years since I'd last been there. The red shutters and gray wood shingle siding looked the same as I remembered. I knew the inside would smell of lemon polish, and everything would be spotless and scrubbed.

Without seeing it, I knew the old back deck would be the same: weathered but sturdy and always covered in sand. I could picture Dad grilling hot dogs and sipping beer while Mom and I watched the waves crash on the shore. I had hoped coming here would be a distraction, but memories of Dad continued to flood my mind.

My stomach ached as I remembered the heavy black dress I wore to Dad's funeral on that scorching day in Phoenix. The air was sizzling, too hot. I'd had to take deep breaths to keep from passing out. Although a canopy shaded the gravesite, the temperature was over 100 degrees. I ached with grief that I couldn't at least see Dad one last time—to make sure it was really him who'd died in that horrible accident. The burning car wreck left his body unidentifiable. The funeral home cremated what was left of his remains.

As I followed the light through the surf, the sea surged with a rolling wave that knocked me over. It was as if something had stirred below the ocean and was rising from the deep. I threw my hands out to break my fall but landed in the shallows on my butt. I sat motionless in the surf, shivering in my wet clothes.

Feeling around in the wet sand, I caught my hand in a clump of green kelp. As I groped around in the mess,

I came across something ridged and firm. Gripping the edges, I pulled it from the murky water. It was a large conch shell covered with vibrant bands of purples, pinks, and blues.

I stumbled to my feet. A shiver ran through me as the icy waves lapped against my bare legs. My mind flashed to Dad's shell collection from this same beach. He'd built a glass case for them in my bedroom back in Phoenix. My fingers trembled as I held the shell, tears dripping off my chin and onto its surface.

The colorful stripes on the conch swirled around and around, shooting rays of color . . . faster, faster . . . mesmerizing me. The entire shell glowed and swirled like a multicolored circle of light. Then, the shell exploded into a fiery ball, and what felt like a lightning bolt shot through my body. I screamed, and the shell jumped out of my hand and landed in the sand. Stunned, I fell back on my butt again. The pulsing ceased, and the vibrant colors faded. The shell lay silently in the sand. I was unable to move; darkness covered me. My heart thumped in my chest. A man's voice echoed in my head . . .

Keep me safe.
I am vulnerable. Take me with you.
I am in your hands. Do not forsake me.
Rescue me from this dark place . . .

"Who's there? Dad? Is that you? Dad? Do you need help—Daddy—are you OK? Please—is that you? I love you, Daddy! Dad!"

Something in the dense, unmoving air made my father's voice seem to come from far away. I opened my eyes. The fog was lifting, and the sun beamed through. Squawking gulls soared in the blue sky above.

I pulled myself up and sat huddled in the damp sand, brushing it off my shorts. Strangely, my clothes were dry. I reached out for the shell with trembling fingers, but remembering the shock, I jerked my hand away. I tapped the shell with my toe to make sure it wouldn't zap me again. It remained dark and still. My finger traced the spires of the conch, and the strange light didn't return. So I snatched it up and trudged back home through the chilly sand.

I found my way to the steps of Nana's weathered deck and sat down. Something had changed, but I couldn't say what. The waves breaking against the shore sounded the same. The breeze still smelled of salt and kelp. The summer sun glimmered through the receding mist, just like before. I couldn't quite put my finger on it, but something wasn't right.

What had happened out there? Was it Dad? Why would he contact me after all this time? Was he OK? He'd mentioned a dark place. Could he be trapped somewhere between here and wherever you go when you die?

CHAPTER 2

THE REUNION

Above my head, on Nana's deck, a fake spider plant hung between driftwood and beach-glass mobiles. Sunlight struck the colorful glass that spun in the breeze. Emerald, sapphire, and gold reflected off the rafters of the deck. When I set foot on the deck, I stashed the shell inside the plant for safekeeping and inched open the sliding glass door.

The aroma of bacon frying and rattling dishes in the kitchen sent me in that direction. Sunlight streamed through the bay window, illuminating jars of homemade canned goods on the shelves. Nana, wearing a tie-dyed t-shirt and jeans, was leaning over a skillet. Her gray braids hung precariously over the hot grease.

"Nana, be careful. Your hair will catch on fire."

Her sweet lined face beamed. "Don't worry, dear. I've been doing this a long time. Breakfast will be ready soon."

I opened my mouth to answer and threw up.

Nana grabbed a towel off the counter, ran over, and wiped my mouth. "Are you sick, Skye? What's wrong, honey?"

I took the cloth from her and dabbed the front of my shirt. "I don't know what happened. I'm going upstairs to wash up." Instead, thinking my nerves had to do with the shell, I ran out to the deck and snatched it from the plant. Upstairs, I kicked the door shut and pulled out my old red backpack from the closet. I rolled the shell in one of my old t-shirts and stuffed the wad inside. I put the pack back in the closet.

A tap at the door made me jump. Mom stuck her head in. "Nana told me you threw up. Is something wrong?"

I wanted to blurt out that something had been wrong for a long time. But I didn't. "I'm fine," I said.

Mom stood in the doorway with her arms crossed over her chest. "Do you want to go to the beach today? I can be ready soon."

"OK," I said, with a pang in my chest. I would rather be back to being my mother's daughter today than check out why the strange shell spoke to me with what I thought was Dad's voice.

I'd never really given myself time to mourn my dad. All my time was reserved for Mom. She had withdrawn into herself, reverting to a state of needing constant care and assurance. More than anything, I wanted her to take me in her arms and tell me she loved me and that she cared. I wanted to hug her close and cry my heart out for Dad. But since Dad's death, she'd never acknowledged my pain, only her own selfish needs.

All she ever cared about anymore was her pills, and now it seemed she was attempting to reach out to me. Maybe spending time together at the beach would make her realize that I also needed attention. After all, she wasn't the only one who was grieving. So I was willing to give her a second chance.

I skipped breakfast, trying not to trigger another nausea attack. Out on the deck, I waited for Mom. She always took her time getting ready. The beach was no longer deserted. A colorful array of umbrellas and towels covered the sand. I spent the time watching two young girls collect seashells. Their laughter echoed in my ears, reminding me of my younger days here when Dad was alive.

When Mom finally showed up, I grabbed a beach blanket and a couple of towels. Since we hadn't eaten breakfast, Nana packed snacks and drinks into a red cooler with ice. I hefted everything into my arms. Mom was bobbing and weaving. She didn't seem steady on her feet—something I was used to.

The salty air whipped across my face as I stepped off the deck. I trudged through the sand carrying all our stuff, feeling like a human coat rack, while Mom did her best to keep up. Finally, we found a spot away from the crowd and spread the blanket. Then I ran off to test the water.

The waves rolled over my legs, and I shivered as I stared out into the endless Pacific, watching the sunbeams dancing off the water. I'd forgotten how beautiful it was here. I ventured farther into the icy waters and caught my breath. Then, behind me, I heard something. Suddenly, a splash of water hit my face, blurring my vision. I wiped the stinging salt from my eyes. A football bobbed in the waves in front of me.

The sun glistening on the water temporarily blinded me. Then I saw him, just a few yards away. Strange, I could swear no one had been there a few minutes ago.

A tall, tanned guy, around my age, with short, thick brown hair shot me a lazy smile. "Sorry for splashing you."

I snatched the ball out of the water and tossed it his way.

"Thanks." He grinned with perfect teeth and sharp brown eyes.

I figured he must work out because he had a really nice chest. I wondered how running my fingers across his ridged muscles would feel. What? What was I thinking? I looked away, flustered.

He moved closer and looked at me like he thought I was pretty.

I backed up a step, still embarrassed he'd caught me staring. Something about him seemed familiar. Wait, wait! I knew him. Paul! The kid who used to pick on me. He'd called me names when we were kids and stomped on my sandcastles. I'd hated him. No longer shy, I pulled myself up, crossing my arms over my chest. "You don't remember me? Skye. The little girl you used to bully."

Redness crept across his face. "Skye Conner? Is that you? You look different, filled out . . . I mean developed . . . grown . . . um . . . bigger . . . um . . . taller. You know?" He bit his lower lip and gazed into the water.

I had to suppress a smile; his goofy expression was cute.

He sucked in a breath, and his eyes met mine. "You finally came back after all this time."

I let out a breath and relaxed my shoulders. "Mom and I are staying with Nana for the summer."

"I was sorry to hear about your dad." He looked away.

"Thanks." I sighed and changed the subject. "I can't believe it's been five years since I was here last."

He ran his fingers through his thick hair and raised an eyebrow. "Yeah, back then, your ribs stuck out, and you had skinny legs."

"Who are you to talk? The last time I saw you, your scrawny butt couldn't hold up your shorts."

"Touché." He smiled and cupped his hand across the water, splashing me. "Want to go for a swim?"

I wanted to wring his neck, but I splashed him back. "Only if you catch me up on what's happening around here."

We swam and talked about the old days and lost track of time. Finally, after about an hour, I suggested we get back to shore. He asked if I wanted to take a walk up to the pier, and I agreed. His face lit up. He reached out to touch my cheek, and my body tensed. I thought he was going to kiss me, and I might have let him do it, but the moment passed. I think he knew it because he pulled away.

We waded to shore, and I headed toward Mom.

She was asleep on the blanket. Her face looked relaxed and peaceful. I wondered if she ever had bad dreams, but I couldn't ask. She would only refuse to talk about it.

I shook her. "Mom, wake up."

She raised her head, peering at me through squinty eyes. "What time is it?"

"Around two. Do you remember Paul, one of the kids I played with when we visited Nana?

"Vaguely . . ." she mumbled, squinting at Paul, massaging her temples.

"We're going for a walk. Let's get the stuff back to the house."

"I can manage," she said.

"No, Mom. I have to get dressed. Didn't you hear anything I said?"

Mom looked up from the blanket and blinked. "I don't want to go for a walk."

I shook my head. "Paul and I are going for a walk. You're going home."

Mom stood and stumbled. I grabbed her arm, and she laughed and slapped my shoulder. I was embarrassed that Paul had to see her this way. She couldn't pull herself together, and it wore on me. Bringing her here, away from Arizona, hadn't changed a thing.

Paul stepped forward, looking serious. "You help your mom get back. I'll grab the stuff."

Back at the house, Paul waited outside while I went upstairs to change. I rummaged through the tops hanging in my closet. Finally, I decided on blue shorts and one of my favorite white cotton tops with lace trim.

Downstairs, in the kitchen, Mom's beach bag lay open on the table. A jar of face cream had fallen out. I bent down to put it back, and something rattled inside. Curious, I unscrewed the lid, and an assortment of pills spilled across the table.

No wonder she was stumbling. She couldn't spend one day with me without drugs. Disgusted, I rounded up the pills, tossed the container back in the bag, and stormed out of the house.

Paul was waiting for me outside. He looked so athletic, a big change from that skinny, awkward kid.

I was still fuming about Mom and the pills, but I forced a smile. "I'm sorry about my mom. She hasn't been herself since Dad died."

He shrugged his muscular shoulders. "She's been through a lot. So have you."

I hated having to discuss my mother's problems with anyone. It was embarrassing having to be the grown-up.

So I tried to cover up her behavior the best I could. It was easy at home but impossible in a public place. I should have told Paul I'd meet him somewhere else.

Since he'd already witnessed Mom's performance, I had nothing to lose by asking him over to the house. "Would you like to come over for dinner sometime? Nana's a great cook."

"I've helped your Nana with repairs and stuff around the house. She makes me lunch when I'm working. That woman could open a five-star restaurant. Sure, I'll come; just give me a heads up."

"Nana didn't mention that you helped her."

"Maybe it slipped her mind."

We crested the bluff that led to the pier and passed a bait-and-tackle shop. Inside, a group of men stood around the counter chatting. Gulls swooped down at tourists eating in the open food court. An older woman in a bright pink Hawaiian muumuu and yellow Crocs waved her hot dog in the air to shoo away a bird, but it grabbed the wiener in its beak and flew away. She swore and threw the bun in the trash.

Watching Paul crack up made me laugh.

CHAPTER 3

THE REAPER

The sun was setting by the time I got back to the cottage. I peered out the sliding door onto the deck. Mom and Nana were in lounge chairs, talking. By the expression on Nana's face, it looked like a serious conversation. They didn't notice me, so I went upstairs to my room and closed the door. I took the pack off the closet shelf and pulled the shell out.

It pulsated in my hand. I stretched out on the bed and placed the conch on my chest, admiring the colors. I brought it to my ear and listened for the sound of the sea, but silence was all I heard. Inside, it twisted around in a spiral pattern, growing smaller and smaller. I couldn't shake the notion that the shell was somehow connected to Dad.

I put the shell back and went downstairs. Nana was at the sink washing dishes while Mom sat at the kitchen table silently, staring at her hands folded in her lap. Mouthwatering aromas of garlic and spaghetti sauce simmering in a pot on the stove filled the air.

Nana slid me a sideways glance as she dried a bowl. "How was your afternoon?"

"I ran into Paul Lucerno on the beach today. He said he does work for you." I sat down at the table.

"He's turned into quite a hunk, hasn't he?" Nana winked at me.

Mom scowled, returning to earth. "I'd appreciate it if you didn't talk like that around Skye."

Nana's back stiffened and she slammed a pot on the counter. Then she stormed over to the table, pulled out a chair, and sat across from Mom. "What do you care about Skye?" Nana said. "When my son died, you decided caring hurt too much. Since then, you never stopped grieving over your dead husband and forgot about the living."

Mom reeled back in her chair like Nana had slapped her. "How dare you speak to me like that!" Mom gasped.

"Skye is not a child. She is a young woman. Three generations of women sit at this table. You and I have not only lost our husbands, but I also lost a son. Don't you dare scare her away from finding love. She has every right to enjoy the happiness we once had. Death is a part of life. Enjoy the ride while you can. The Reaper can show up on our doorstep at any moment." Nana sat back and crossed her arms, daring Mom to challenge her.

Mom looked away, sulking, staring out the window at something far beyond the California coast.

Nana turned to me and smiled. "How about inviting Paul to dinner sometime? He's been a godsend to me around here."

"I'm sure he's been paid for his efforts," Mom interjected.

Nana's eyes narrowed, cautioning Mom. "I count on his help."

"I already mentioned dinner to him," I said.

Nana smiled. "Perfect. Let me know when he's available, and I'll make a roast."

After supper, Nana put an old rock album on her turntable, and we sat outside. Nana and Mom drank a glass of wine on the deck. I sat on the rail and sipped a Coke. It wasn't long before I got sleepy, so I excused myself and went up to my room.

I went to the closet, took the shell out of the pack, and put it on the dresser. Then I undressed and slipped into bed. Music played through the open window. The singer sang something about the pills that Mother gives you. Always the damn pills.

The seashell glowed, lighting up the wall behind the dresser. I was curious but too exhausted to climb out of bed and check it out. Spellbound, I closed my eyes . . .

Our thoughts and dreams are one.
I sense your suffering, your loneliness, your loss.
Help me, and I will help you . . .

I woke, drenched in sweat, and tossed off the covers. Dad was trying to communicate with me again. What does he want? Shivering, I rolled onto my side and pulled the quilt up over my head.

CHAPTER 4

SUSPICIONS

A week passed, and Paul and I spent every day swimming, body surfing, and getting to know each other. Paul finally came to dinner. He was a perfect gentleman, polite and attentive. Nana did most of the talking. Mom silently pushed peas around on her plate and went to bed early. The roast was delicious; Paul went for seconds.

The following morning, Paul and I strolled across the beach. He wore a gray Under Armor t-shirt that clung to his chiseled chest. It was hard to keep my eyes off his body. I was falling for him. Hard to believe that this was the same creepy kid that caused me pain.

Paul turned to me. "Your mom's changed. I remember her laughing and riding her bike around town. You guys were always doing family stuff."

The breeze blew my hair across my face, and I pushed it back. "When Dad was alive, they had a lot of happy times here at the beach. Mom and Dad would sit on the deck in the evening and drink beer. She laughed and joked with Dad like a girl on a date. After the funeral, Mom started taking all these pills. Now, she acts like a zombie. I hate her for not being stronger."

Paul silently stared ahead, and I wondered if I had ruined the mood. I wanted his opinion about Mom's addiction, some insight. But on the other hand, maybe he didn't want to hear about my problems.

He glanced my way every few moments. I couldn't read him and didn't want to press for an answer. His indifference made me feel embarrassed for confiding in him.

We drifted along the dock as tourists went about their lives, riding bikes, strolling, and chatting on the pier. I wasn't paying much attention; I was still wrestling with Paul's reaction, or lack of, to my confession. The smell of corn dogs permeated the air, reminding me that I was hungry.

We passed a small shop with a metal sign hanging over the outside service window that read *Shores Edge Frosty Treats*. Brightly colored cartoon-like smiling swirling cones with big round eyes advertised *Twenty Delicious Flavors*. The colorful sign creaked on rusted hinges in the sea breeze.

I swallowed a lump in my throat. Most evenings, after supper, while Mom and Nana cleared the dishes, Dad and I would walk to this same shop. We'd sit on the pier, eating our cones, watching the sunset, talking and laughing. I wouldn't trade those precious moments for anything.

Inside the shop, nothing had changed. The same old fishing nets stretched across the ceiling holding dusty starfish, colored glass balls, and sea-polished driftwood. Dad would lift me in his arms so I could touch the starfish.

A tall, attractive girl in a bright pink top and white shorts stood behind the counter. Short, spiky dark hair complimented her pretty heart-shaped face.

"How about an ice cream?" I reached out, took Paul's hand, and pulled him toward the entrance under a red-and-white canopy.

Paul pulled back and frowned. "What about a burger and a malt?"

I tugged at his arm. "Dad used to bring me here. I want to taste the ice cream again. We can grab a burger later."

I walked inside with Paul in tow and a scowl crossed the server's face. "Can I help you?"

I stepped forward. "Single vanilla cone, please."

"Chocolate," Paul mumbled. He stood back, rubbing his palms against his thighs, gazing at the ceiling.

As the girl scooped, she kept giving Paul sideways glances. Finally, she handed me the cones. I turned to give Paul his ice cream. He reluctantly took it, but he didn't look happy. Was he upset because I didn't want lunch? I was beginning to wonder if he was always this moody. He was acting childish, so I went outside while he paid.

We drifted along the pier, licking our cones—tasty, but not as good as when Dad and I had them. I held the napkin to my lips to catch the drippings melting in the hot sun and studied Paul's sharp features. He seemed to care for me; the way he looked at me, his compliments. We liked hanging out, or I did.

Still angered by his behavior, I blurted out, "You never answered me about the issue with my mom. You say you like being with me, but you're distant. I tell you about what's going on in my life, but you don't share yours. And why were you so mad when I wanted ice cream? I thought you'd changed, but you're acting like the jerk you used to be when you wrecked my sandcastles."

Paul sighed. "When you came back, I saw you in the water in your blue bikini. I threw the ball at you so I could meet you. Then I realized who you were. I thought you might hate me for teasing you when we were young. I only did it because I liked you. It was my dumb kid's way of making you notice me."

He did all those mean things to me because he liked me? What a stupid way to show it.

Paul placed his hands on my shoulders and studied me with his piercing brown eyes. My insides went jittery.

He said, "Skye, I'm sorry you're having a hard time. What happened to your dad, the problems with your mom?" He paused, then continued, "My dad abandoned us a few years ago and ran off with his receptionist. My mom sucked it up and acted like it didn't hurt. She fooled my little brother, but I knew different."

I took a moment to think about what he said. Maybe I was being too hard on him. "I don't expect you to have the answers. Just be there for me. No one has been there to support me since Dad died. Now I have you and Nana. And I want Mom to get help."

We walked home, reliving the times when we were kids. Paul reminded me that I wasn't totally innocent in our battles. Like the time I bopped him on the head with my pail when he stomped on my sandcastle, and he had to get stitches.

When we parted, Paul said he'd come by at ten the following day, but he didn't show. I was restless by noon, so I hiked down to the shore, staying in sight of the cottage in case he showed up. After that, I spent another hour pacing between the beach and the house, glancing at my cell phone every few minutes.

Tired of waiting, I went up to the pier and wandered around, searching the crowd for any sign of him. I was acting like a lovesick schoolgirl, but my pride wouldn't let me call him or go to his house. If I accidentally ran into him at the pier, it wouldn't be like stalking.

At the ice cream shop, the same pretty girl was serving an older man wearing loud Bermuda shorts and clunky sandals. She looked at me, frowned, and dropped the cone.

"Hey, girly, pay attention to what you're doing," the man complained.

"I'll make you another one," she said.

Her eyes bore into me while I waited. Finally, she handed the guy his ice cream. He snatched the cone and shuffled away.

She turned to me. "Vanilla cone, right?"

I nodded.

"Where's your boyfriend, the tall, good-looking guy you were with yesterday?"

"Do you know Paul?" I asked.

"I've seen him around," she said.

"Was he here today?"

"No, not today. By the way, I'm Karly."

"I'm Skye," I said, gazing up at the dusty starfish trapped in the nets . . .

You took me out of my dark place in the ocean . . .

"Are you on vacation?" she said.

Her voice brought me out of my trance. "I'm staying at my grandma's place for the summer."

"Here you go." Her hand was trembling as she handed it over. I wrapped the cone in a napkin and took a lick. "Thanks, it tastes great." I handed her a five. She opened the register and deposited the bill.

"How long have you known Paul?" she asked as she gave me my change.

"Since we were kids, from previous visits here."

"Where are you from?"

Her questions were making me uneasy. "Phoenix."

She drummed her nails on the counter. "If you're smart, you'll steer clear of Paul." Her eyes narrowed, and her lips curled into a smirk. "He'll lie to you, break your heart. I should know—he broke mine."

I backed up. "What are you talking about?"

Karly's once pretty face turned hard. "Paul loved me before he started hanging out with you. Stay away from him."

Her words sent me reeling. I staggered out of the shop, dropping my cone on the pier. It couldn't be true—she had to be nuts—obsessed with Paul. I glanced back. She stood glaring at me with a grimace on her lips. I stumbled down the pier, trembling. I leaned against the railing at the end of the dock to catch my breath. A flock of seagulls dived in and out of the water, searching for food. I turned back to see if Karly was watching me, but she was busy with a customer.

When I got home, I felt sick to my stomach. In the kitchen, I chugged a glass of water. Nana had left a note on the counter saying she was driving into town for groceries. Mom was passed out on the couch in the living room, her face planted in a cushion. Her wrinkled blouse rode up, exposing a bloated white stomach like the belly of a dead fish. Mom was out of control, a complete mess, and I had no idea how to fix her.

I couldn't stay in the house and watch her sleep it off. I needed air—I needed to know if Paul was unfaithful or if Karly was a liar. Just when I thought things were getting better, they were getting worse.

The sound of someone rapping on the sliding door startled me. It was Paul. I wondered if Karly had called him. I felt like leaving him out there and hiding in my room, but I shoved the door open and went outside.

"Where have you been?" I was unable to curb the venom in my voice. "I waited for you all afternoon. You could have at least called."

"My mom went out with friends. I told her I'd spend time with Jeff—you remember, my brother. I was going to call you, but we started playing video games, and I forgot."

"It's not just that you didn't call." I was shaking, unable to control my anger. "There's more to it than that."

"What's wrong, Skye?"

I clenched my fists, and tears ran down my cheeks. "Karly, at the ice cream shop. She said you loved each other, and I'm in the way. Is that true?"

Paul paced back and forth across the deck, repeatedly slamming his fist into his palm. "She's a liar. She's sick. Believe me. Karly has mental problems. She's been stalking me."

His anger was scaring me. Was he mad because she told me about them, or was I jumping the gun by not giving him the benefit of the doubt? Was Karly crazy, jealous—actually a stalker? I was so confused.

"I don't know what to think," I said. You'd better leave. We'll talk about it later."

Paul clenched his fists. "Karly won't get away with this. I'll make her sorry. Catch you later."

I stood on the deck, shivering, watching Paul race down the beach. His last words echoed in my mind. *I'll make her sorry . . .*

The sound of an engine coming up the drive signaled Nana's arrival. The old green VW Bus pulled up to the garage, and the door flew open. "Skye, help me unload," she called.

After the groceries were out of the van and put away in the kitchen, I slipped away to my room.

I closed the door and leaned against it. Once the tears started, I couldn't hold them back. I picked the shell off the dresser and stumbled over to the bed. Wet tears trickled onto the shell, which sent off strange lights and vibrations. The throbbing grew stronger and louder. It sounded like a helicopter coming in for a landing. I resisted the urge to hurl it across the room. My head pounded; I wanted to scream. Louder and louder, closer, and closer . . .

I threw my hands over my ears to drive the noise out of my head. Hot currents of air whipped around my body, and with a cry of terror, I fell to the floor.

There, I lay, listening to the sudden silence in the room. What the hell just happened?

CHAPTER 5

THE LEGACY

The following morning, I left the house early to confront Karly. I needed to find out if Paul was innocent. As I neared the ice cream shop, I caught a glimpse of Karly's back through the front window. She was busy restocking the supplies. When she turned and hoisted a carton onto the counter, I gasped. Karly's pretty face was swollen and bruised.

Unnoticed, I turned and raced home.

When I saw an ambulance in the driveway, I forgot about Karly. I stopped in my tracks, breathing hard. No, not Nana. Had something happened to Nana? I ran across the beach and reached the deck; my heart thumped in my chest. I grabbed the handle on the sliding door to pull it open. Nana stumbled out and barred my way. Tears blurred her eyes.

"Skye, don't go in there." Nana reached out and hugged me to her bosom, choking on her words. "Your mom overdosed. I found her a little while ago. She didn't make it. I'm so sorry, dear." She held me tighter.

"What, Nana?" I pulled away. Her words were jumbled. I looked at her face, not fully processing what she'd just said.

Nana took hold of my shoulders, squeezed, and looked me straight in the eyes. "Your mother overdosed on pills last night."

"What? How could she?" I stammered. "I told her the pills would kill her, that she needed help." My tears fell in frustration and anger that Mom hadn't listened.

Nana rubbed my shoulders and looked into my eyes. "Don't blame yourself, Skye. You did all you could to help her, but she wouldn't listen. I should have done more. Insist she see a professional."

"What happens now? How are we going to get through this?" I wiped the tears from my eyes.

Nana took my hands in hers. "One day, one moment at a time, whatever it takes. I'm here for you. Whatever you need from me, I'm here. You have been through so much. First, losing your dad, my son. Now your mom. You don't deserve this pain, this loss, all within less than a year." She drew me close in a tight embrace. "You can count on me, honey," she whispered.

Safely wrapped in Nana's arms, I felt shielded from the world's pain, disappointment, and cruelty. My tears flowed. God, I loved this sweet, kind, strong woman.

"Skye, I want you to stay out here on the deck. The police will be here shortly, and the coroner." She studied my face. "They won't move her body without an investigation."

"Where is she?"

"In bed. She passed away in the night. There was nothing I could do when I went to wake her up." Nana kept her eyes on me, seeking a reaction. "If you don't want to hear this, I won't talk about it."

"I need to know. When Dad died, people whispered. They treated me like I was fragile. They kept me in the dark, afraid I would fall apart. Then, after the service, they went back to their lives. Mom couldn't cope. She fell apart and depended on me. Please don't shut me out, Nana. I need you to treat me like an adult."

A sheriff's car and a white van came down the road and pulled into the driveway. I took a deep breath and shuddered. Nana stood frozen in place as we watched them approach the house. Finally, the doors flew open, and an officer exited the cruiser while two women got out of the van.

Nana moved into action. "After I talk to them, I'll bring you a nice cup of hot chamomile tea."

My shaking hand moved to brush away the tightness in my chest. "Oh, Nana, I don't need any tea."

"It's what I need to do." Nana squeezed my shoulder. "I'll be right back." She turned and went inside to meet them.

I sat at the table, put my head in my hands, and drew a deep breath. "Mom, why couldn't you be tougher? I tried to be the perfect daughter. I realized you were hurting.

Why couldn't you suck it up and be there for me? Before Dad died, you were vibrant and alive, doing what you could to hold our family together. What happened to you? I have been angry at you for so long. Now that you're gone, I need to forgive you for your weakness."

Nana came out carrying a mug. "Here, honey, drink this. The police are wrapping up their investigation. They'll transport your mom soon. You wait outside until they are done."

"I don't need to hide out here." I set the mug on the table, stood up, and followed Nana into the house.

Inside, the women from the van carried a stretcher with Mom's body draped in a black cloth down the stairs. I gasped, and my knees buckled. They wheeled her past me and then out the front door.

I followed them outside and stood on the front porch, motionless, feeling totally alone. A crowd had gathered on the road, gawking, and speaking in hushed voices about the tragedy at Nana's house. My face flushed with anger that they were treating my misfortune like a circus show. Then my attention was drawn back to the van with Mom's body as it backed out of the driveway and slowly disappeared down the road.

After everyone had left, Nana went upstairs to clean Mom's room. Word travels fast in a small town. It wasn't long before Paul dropped by to offer his condolences. He couldn't look me in the eye. I didn't know what to say. So many thoughts and emotions ran through my mind.

I narrowed my eyes and studied his expression. "I saw Karly this morning."

"Karly? Did she come by?" His face looked more perplexed than guilty.

"I saw her on the pier this morning."

"What did she say?"

"Nothing, I just saw her." I didn't know what there was to say. So much had happened; words escaped me. Everything was such a mess. "Listen, Paul. I'm upset and confused right now."

He leaned in to kiss my cheek, and I cringed. "I just need time to think," I said.

He stepped back, but I could see the hurt in his eyes. "If you need anything, call. I'll come right over."

I walked Paul to the door, leaned against the frame, and watched him head for the beach. His head was down, and his shoulders were slumped. He looked like a broken man, but I couldn't feel too much pity for him. If he'd done that to Karly's face and could look me in the eye without a hint of remorse, then he was either innocent—or a monster.

That evening, Nana and I sat silently across from each other, picking at our grilled cheese sandwiches and tomato soup. Finally, Nana put down her spoon and lifted her chin. "Skye, I want you to stay here and live with me. I'll help you sell the house in Phoenix. It will give you a little money. I want you here until you figure out what you want to do with your life."

"Oh, Nana. I would love that. You're all I have." I started to cry. It touched my heart that she wanted me.

In the days following Mom's death, I could feel her presence in the house. I don't know if I was just used to having her around or if it was something mystical, out of my control. Nana and I searched Mom's room in case she'd left a note. After carefully rummaging through her things, all we found were more bottles of pills. It gave me no comfort to flush them down the toilet. The damage was done. It was too late; nothing would bring Mom back. Nana ordered a new bed for Mom's room and had the old one hauled away. She said it was bad karma to keep it.

Mom was cremated. We planned on having a small private service and scattering her ashes in the Pacific. Mom had a sister and brother who both lived in the Midwest. We phoned them about Mom's passing. They hadn't seen each other in many years. We told them there wouldn't be a service for Mom. After the calls, the sympathy cards arrived. They carried an underlying relief that they wouldn't have to travel to California for a funeral.

Each day, Paul came by to be supportive. I was friendly but distant. Neither of us mentioned Karly. I didn't know what to make of her bruises, but I planned to investigate after Mom was laid to rest. I still had feelings for him and wanted to believe in his innocence.

All through this hard time, I kept having strange dreams. In them, I heard Dad's voice pleading for release from a dark place and saw a psychedelic slideshow of the universe and the bottom of the sea. At least they didn't include Mom. I wanted to tell Nana about the dreams, but I kept my mouth shut. It wasn't the time to go psycho on her.

The morning we cast Mom into the sea was bittersweet. I expected a dismal, foggy send-off, but the sun shone in a clear royal blue sky. Paul joined our procession. I carried the urn that held Mom's ashes. Nana and Paul followed me single file through the sparkly sand to cast Mom into the ocean. We trailed across the beach toward the jetty, where waves crashed against the rocks. Finally, we reached the point and stood at the water's edge.

Nana broke the silence. "Skye, do you want to say something?"

All morning, I'd thought about what I should say, but couldn't I come up with anything that felt right. So I just spoke what was on my mind. "Mom, I'm sorry that it had to come to this. I love you and wish I could have done more to help you with your depression. I only pray that you are finally at peace." Tears filled my eyes, clouding my vision.

Standing on the rocks above the Pacific, I removed the cover of the urn, reached in, then tossed her ashes into the air. A breeze carried Mom's remains across the bay until they floated on the surface of the blue-green water. Nana said a prayer. It was short and sweet, but I don't remember the verses. I climbed down the rocks to the surf and doused the urn with water. Afterward, we trailed home in silence.

Nana arranged a Celebration of Life buffet back at the house with cold cuts, hoagie rolls, salads, and slices of cheesecake from the deli. Besides Paul's mom, Carolyn, and his brother, Jeff, a few of Nana's friends showed up. It was enough. Although it was a celebration for Mom, it brought back images of Dad's service.

I remembered it well. Mom was making a scene in the crowded reception hall, crying so hard she was shaking. Her performance was getting her plenty of sympathy. Leave it to Mom to divert all the attention to herself while Nana and I sat quietly mourning at the table reserved for family. I was angry and scared that Dad was gone, but so mad at Mom's behavior that I couldn't shed a tear. She took center stage and pushed me into the background.

Dad had always made sure we had what we needed, so Mom didn't have to work. Whenever Mom and I argued, he intervened, usually in my favor. After he died, the insurance money from Dad's accident provided enough for us to stay in the house and pay the bills. I often wondered: had there been no money and Mom was forced to get a job, would she have become addicted to the pills? Mom didn't try—not even for me. She just gave up.

Nana carried a plate over and set it on the table, bringing me out of my thoughts of Dad's funeral and back to the present. "Skye, eat something. You didn't have any breakfast." She hovered over me, frowning.

A wedge of some sandwich, a sliver of pickle, and three piles of assorted salads smothered in mayonnaise stared me in the face. "I'm not hungry. I lost my appetite."

"How about a glass of milk? I'll bring you one."

"Oh, Nana, I'll get it. You don't have to serve me. I need something to do other than just sit here. You go and make sure everyone is fed." I got up, kicked my chair aside, and headed for the fridge to get a drink.

Later that afternoon, I walked Paul to the door. He hugged me, and I froze. Paul awkwardly pulled away and backed out the door. Tears ran down my cheeks as I watched him go. I suddenly realized the laughs and good times were over with Paul. My heart ached for him, but what happened with Karly wouldn't leave my mind.

CHAPTER 6

SECRETS

The first two weeks after Mom's service, I spent a lot of time on the deck, crying and staring out at the ocean. The guilt and grief of losing both my parents felt suffocating. Being alone, orphaned at eighteen. Thank God for Nana. She stayed by my side and comforted me. We spoke about Mom, Dad, and my plans for a new life here. Back home, I had planned to go to college, but my immediate plans had changed with everything that had happened. Each day, Paul called to check on me. I was always polite to him but brief.

I made a list of three things I needed to do right away. One, find out the truth about Karly and Paul. Two, figure out what the shell had to do with my weird dreams. And three, get a job, even if it was part-time. I couldn't sit around Nana's all day with nothing to do.

In the kitchen, I helped Nana with the dinner dishes. The sliding glass door stood open. The ocean breeze caught the beach glass mobiles on the deck, and they played a tinkling tune. It was still early, but I was exhausted. Upstairs, I undressed, crawled into bed in my underwear, and turned out the light. The shell on the dresser cast an eerie glow of swirling colors around the room. I wanted to get out of bed and check it out, but I was hypnotized. Finally, drowsiness blanketed me, my heavy lids closed, and I drifted off . . .

A prisoner at the bottom of the vast ocean. A discarded shell protects my life form. Entombed, waiting to be free of my dark prison. I seek your help locating a host to enter the mind as the life force begins to leave that individual. Then I will be free of this dark existence.

I must find a host . . .

My eyes opened to morning sunlight streaming through the windows—another dream. Tears filled my eyes. I wanted so much for the voice to be Dad's. But deep down, I knew it wasn't him. But whoever it was, I wasn't afraid, only curious. Maybe it didn't scare me because I had nothing to lose now that both my parents were gone.

I got out of bed and stumbled to the bathroom. In the shower, the hard spray invigorated me. The water turned cold, and I dried off and threw on a pair of shorts and a t-shirt. I picked up the shell from the dresser. The colors glistened and glowed as I twisted it in my hands.

Each ridge and stripe changed colors with each twirl. The shell mesmerized and soothed me.

I grabbed a flashlight from the nightstand and shined it inside the shell. The light wrapped around and folded back on itself, growing smaller and smaller.

Next, I brought the shell to my lips and spoke into the opening: "Hello." Then I brought it back to my ear. A faint "Hello" echoed from inside.

Startled, I dropped the shell on the bed. It rolled across the quilt and almost fell on the floor. I don't know why I felt edgy; it was only my voice echoing from inside the shell.

I picked it up and set it on the dresser. It seemed content between the framed pictures—one of Mom and Dad and me and the other of Paul and me. He'd taken a selfie of us on the beach and printed it out for me. I turned and glanced at my family on the dresser as I stepped out the door.

In the kitchen, the smell of coffee permeated the air. I poured a mug and inhaled the aroma. Sipping the hot brew, I wandered out on the deck. In the garden, Nana watered plants wearing an orange and yellow tie-dyed shirt. I smiled. A blast from the past; that's what she'd say. I drained the cup and called to Nana: "I'm going into town. Can I borrow your bike?"

Nana turned off the flow to the nozzle. "Why don't you take the van?"

I patted my thighs. "I could use the exercise."

Nana laughed. "Go ahead, wear yourself out. Have a good time, honey."

I asked around and found out where Karly lived. A kid that worked at the bait shop told me. I didn't want to talk to her at work—too many interruptions.

I pedaled down the driveway into the street and cruised toward Karly's house. If she wasn't home, I had nothing to lose but fresh air and exercise. Most of the way there, the streets were level, but I had to maneuver a steep grade for about a quarter mile that got me panting and made my legs ache. Once I reached the top, I lifted my feet off the pedals and flew down the hill. I gripped the handlebars hard and let the wind whip across my face all the way down to the curb in front of Karly's house.

Straddling the seat, I could see paint flaking off the wood siding, shingles curling up off the roof, and weeds growing out of the cracks in the driveway. I marched up the front steps and knocked on the door. A cat ran out from under a tarp thrown over an old, discarded dresser by the wall, and I stumbled backward.

The door flew open, and Karly blocked the entrance. She stood with her arms crossed just below her breasts. Without makeup, she didn't resemble the girl at the pier. "What do you want?" she snapped.

My knees went weak. "I need to talk to you."

"About what? I already told you everything you need to know."

I peered past her into the dingy living room. A worn brown recliner leaned against the wall next to a saggy couch covered with a gray blanket. An enormous old TV was perched on a metal stand. An overflowing ashtray sat among crushed beer cans and an empty bottle of whiskey on the coffee table.

Karly turned to see what I was gawking at. "HGTV hasn't been by yet," she sneered.

My shoulders tensed and sweat rolled down my temples. "Sorry, but there's something I need to know."

"You want the name of my decorator?"

This wasn't going the way I had planned. I swallowed the panic caught in my throat. "The morning after you told me about Paul, I came to see you at work. You had a black eye and bruises on your face."

"Why do you care?"

"The day before, I spoke to Paul about what you said, and he was furious. He said you lied to me about the whole thing. Then, he took off to confront you about it."

Karly snickered. "You think he hit me? He doesn't have the balls! What a pair you make. You don't trust him, and he lies to you. You belong together." She turned to shut the door.

"Wait!" I held my hand out and blocked the door halfway through its swing. "What happened to your face?"

Karly rounded on me, and I stumbled back, afraid she was going to slap me. "If you must know, it was my dear old dad," she spat. "He has a temper. He's not in line for Father of the Year anytime soon." She turned and slammed the door in my face.

I stood on the porch, shaking. So, Paul hadn't hit her. With a dad like that, no wonder Karly was messed up. I retrieved my bike from the overgrown weeds in the yard and rode home, feeling bad for Karly. But I was also relieved that Paul wasn't responsible for her bruises.

After putting the bike in the garage, I called Paul and asked him to meet me for lunch. I had to be honest and tell him what I suspected.

The Marina Grill on the pier was bustling with the noontime crowd when I entered. The restaurant was popular; it had good food and fantastic views. Wooden tables sat against the walls, and a butcher block bar lined with stools separated the kitchen area. The smell of grilled burgers in the air made my mouth water. Paul waved me over from a table at a window with a panoramic view of the ocean. His gray Nike shirt and dark blue shorts accentuated his muscles. Leave it to Paul to be one of the most handsome guys in the restaurant. I crossed the room and joined him.

A young waiter wearing a blue apron with a yellow embroidered anchor brought water and menus. Colorful sailboats heading out of the marina zipped across the shimmering ocean—quite a change from Arizona's dry, barren desert. Everything about being on the beach was special. Living here wouldn't be hard to take.

I was nervous about what to tell Paul about Karly. I was ashamed of myself for jumping to conclusions but willing to apologize.

"Thanks for meeting me." My legs fidgeted under the table.

"No problem." He reached across the table and brushed my hand.

I pulled it back and placed it in my lap. "Sorry about being so distant. A lot has been going on."

His eyes sought mine through thick dark lashes, making me soften. "Don't apologize. I know what you've been going through."

"You don't know everything." I looked away.

The waiter appeared, and Paul ordered a cheeseburger and fries. I asked for a grilled cheese on sourdough, and we both asked for Cokes. He scribbled on his pad and left.

My fingers gripped the table's edge. "Paul, I have a confession to make. I went to see Karly the morning before I found out that my mom had passed. Karly's face was bruised. She was busy stocking supplies, so she didn't see me. Then I went back to see her again today. She told me her dad hit her."

The muscles under his shirt twitched. "Karly's dad is an abusive drunk. Her mom took off with some guy when Karly was just a kid. Her dad hits her. She works to help support him, and that's how he pays her back. She takes the abuse and refuses to press charges against him. They have a sick codependent relationship."

"I thought *you'd* hit her."

Paul jerked his head back like I had slapped him. "Why would you think that?"

"You were so angry when I mentioned what Karly told me. Then you stormed off to confront her. I thought it had gotten out of hand."

His eyes narrowed, and his face looked angry and hurt. "You think I would hit a girl? Give me more credit than that."

"Well, you used to bully me. So, I didn't know what to expect."

"We were just kids. I never touched you."

"You shoved me off my bike."

"I was playing with you."

"I don't call pushing someone playing. You hurt me and made me cry. Why couldn't you just have brought me candy like a normal boy?"

We sat there, silently staring each other down. Finally, his expression softened. "Look, that was a long time ago. I made a mistake. I didn't mean to mistreat you. Just because I was nasty to you back then, you assumed I beat up Karly. We were both wrong. Can we call a truce?"

I tried to laugh, but it got stuck in my throat.

Paul's brow furrowed. "What's so funny?"

I reached out and traced his forearm on the table with my finger. "We're acting like a couple of kids. Don't you find that funny?"

He took my hand and grinned. "I guess we are. I wish you would have asked me about her bruises. I thought you were still mad at what Karly said about me and her—that you believed her."

"I couldn't bring myself to think about it." I sighed. "Mom's death, the service. I wasn't strong enough to deal with anything else at the time. I'm sorry."

The waiter brought our order. Then, after fussing with the silverware and napkins and refilling our drinks, he disappeared.

Paul leaned in and brushed my cheek. "I don't know if I could be as strong as you. Losing both parents, being away from home and your friends. You have been dealt one blow after the other and haven't given up."

I reached over and took his hand. "Oh, Paul, I'm not strong." Tears blurred my eyes. "It's just that I have nothing to lose now that my parents are both gone."

He squeezed my hand. "Don't say that. You have your Nana and me."

"I know. And believe me, I'm grateful for that." I smiled, pulled my hand away, and dabbed my eyes with my napkin.

The aroma of melted cheddar made me remember that I hadn't eaten breakfast. "Thanks for understanding. Let's eat before it gets cold." I took a bite of my sandwich.

Talking to Paul that day made me realize how much that poor girl was screwed up. Karly wanted Paul. She couldn't have him, so she resorted to telling lies, making me doubt him. I decided I wasn't going to believe anything anyone said unless I saw it with my own eyes. And I wouldn't be getting ice cream anytime soon.

CHAPTER 7

A FALL FROM GRACE

The following week, I strolled along the shoreline. The waves splashed against my ankles as a salty breeze whipped the hair across my face. The rhythm of the waves was hypnotic and calming. My toes pushed into the wet sand as I looked out over the Pacific.

Paul jogged across the sand in black swim trunks. He caught up and threw his arms around my waist, pulling me close. "Want to go swimming?"

"Couldn't we take a walk and explore today? Something different?"

"Let's go up to Hunter's Point. The view is fantastic," he said.

"I've never been up there. That sounds like fun."

"I'll get my pack and meet you at your house."

"OK, I'll be ready."

We gathered our gear and walked about a mile across the beach until we reached the trailhead. The climb up the steep bluff wasn't going to be easy. I was already sweating from trudging through the sand. Readjusting the pack on my shoulders, I wiped the sweat from my brow with a bandana.

"I hope that pack isn't going to be too heavy for you," Paul said.

"I guess I'll find out once we get on the trail."

"If it gets to be too much, I'll carry it for a while."

"I think I'll be all right," I said, and smiled.

As we trudged up the hill, my mind wandered to the odd dreams and the voice inside the shell. I glanced over at Paul; his mouth was moving, but I wasn't paying attention.

"What did you say?"

"I said, are you getting tired? Do you need to rest?" He pointed at some large rocks under a cypress tree. We hiked over and sat on a boulder in the shade. I pulled a water bottle out of my pack, and he did the same. The water cooled my parched throat. The sun reflected off the shimmering blue-green sea below.

Paul turned to me, wiping the sweat from his fore-head. "Is something wrong?"

"I've been having weird dreams."

"Nightmares?"

"No, I wouldn't call them nightmares, but they're creepy." I took another sip. "Someone or something is attempting to contact me. A voice. At first, I thought it was my dad, but now, I'm not so sure."

"What's going on?"

"It's a voice in my head while I sleep. It wants something—release from a dark place. That's why I thought it was Dad, but the more I thought about it . . . it just doesn't make sense."

He put his arm around my shoulder. "They're just dreams. Not real. You woke up."

"It reminds me of those old Freddie Kruger movies. You know, the slasher guy who pops up out of nowhere and gets you when you fall asleep. You can't escape, no matter how much coffee you gulp." I sounded like a nut.

Paul grinned. "Yeah, those movies scared me when I was a kid. But it's fake. Things like that don't happen in real life. We'll figure out what's going on. I won't let anything happen to you. I've got your back."

Nice of him to say, but I didn't think that Paul could protect me from the dreams. They were so otherworldly. I shivered.

"Do you want to go back? We don't have to go to the top."

"No, let's move on. All this exercise will help take my mind off the other stuff."

We pulled on our packs and started up the trail. As we crested the summit, someone was hiking ahead in the distance bundled in a gray sweatshirt with a hood on. It seemed strange that a hiker would wear a hoodie on such a warm day. I tried to get a better look, but the dense foliage blocked my view.

An inviting picnic table sat shaded under an enormous oak. When we reached it, I took my pack off, and stood on top of the table, scanning the area for the mysterious stranger. Not seeing anyone, I turned to the cliff and the breathtaking view of the ocean below.

Meanwhile, Paul followed a dusty path that ended at the cliff. "Skye, come over here; you can see the beach below," he shouted.

"No. I can see it from here. I'm afraid of heights," I hollered back from the table.

"I'll be right back," he waved, then disappeared over the bluff.

"Paul, be careful," I called.

A few minutes later, I heard Paul scream. "Hey! Hey! What the . . . No! Stop! Ahhh . . ."

Then, silence.

"Paul . . . Paul, what's wrong?"

Silence.

I ran to where he'd climbed over the steep ridge. A ledge below led to a narrow path that spanned the cliff. I sucked in my breath and clutched the thick branches of a bush that grew between two boulders on the ridge. Leaning over, I yelled, "Paul . . . Paul! Can you hear me?" Over and over, I screamed his name. He must have fallen and been badly hurt, or worse. And who was he yelling at? That stranger in the hoodie? A cold sensation crept up my spine. I looked around. Not seeing anyone,

I ran back to the table, ripped my phone out of the pack, and dialed 911.

"911, what's your emergency?"

"My friend fell off a cliff. I think someone might have pushed him. I can't see where he is, and I've been calling his name, but he doesn't answer me." I cried.

"Can you tell me your location?"

"I'm on Hunter's Point. It's a bluff above Crescent Bay. Do you know the location?"

"Yes, I have you in our GPS. Wait where you are. Help will arrive soon. You said someone pushed him? Can you identify the person?"

"I didn't see anyone push him. There was a strange person around here when we arrived."

"Are they still there?"

"No, I don't see anyone now."

"Report it to the authorities when they arrive. Can I call you on this number?"

"Yes. I'll be waiting . . . hurry!"

I couldn't just sit there and wait for help to arrive. Wandering over to where I'd last seen Paul, I looked over the precipice, but he wasn't there. I was light-headed and dizzy. My knees began to shake. *Be brave. Do something.*

I grabbed my pack, then slowly eased myself over the edge by clutching at the branches growing out of the side of the cliff. One step at a time, feeling for footholds on the rocks. As I lowered myself down, I was shaking and sweating. I wanted to climb back up, but I had to find Paul. I had to do something, even if it meant I didn't make it. I'd rather be dead than leave him to die alone.

I climbed about fifteen or twenty feet below the cliff and couldn't see him. Brush covered the entire wall of rock, so I pushed on. I seized whatever I could hold, working myself further down the cliff. Finally, I saw a large flat boulder and pulled myself onto it.

My hands were bleeding, and my limbs throbbed. Crawling to the edge, I glanced over. Paul lay on the shelf below, not moving. It was another twenty feet or so to reach him. The rest of the way was hardscrabble. My weight caused the small pebbles under my feet to give way. Nevertheless, adrenaline kept me going; I slid down the rest of the way on my butt until I reached Paul.

His clothes were ripped and covered in blood. He gasped out shallow breaths, but he was alive. "Paul, can you hear me?" No response. I patted his cheek, afraid to move him in case of a back or neck injury. Still no response.

I pulled a water bottle and a bandana from my pack. I drizzled water over the scarf and wiped the blood from his face. After rinsing the blood from the cloth, I rubbed the wet cloth over his dry lips. It was all I could do to keep him comfortable until help arrived.

The sound of helicopter blades brought me around. The craft appeared from behind the bluff. I flagged it down. "Hurry, he's over here," I shouted and waved.

Several cables appeared from the hovering copter. Then, a man and a woman in brown jumpsuits and orange vests descended toward me. Next, another line lowered a basket and backboard. When they reached the ground, they rushed to examine Paul. Then they strapped his body onto the backboard and placed him in the rescue basket for transport to the copter.

One of them strapped me in a harness and attached me to a cable. I ascended to the copter, queasy. I squeezed my eyes shut to keep from throwing up. The closer I got to the helicopter, the louder the roar and thump of the blades . . .

Hands grabbed me, and I was pulled inside the copter and strapped into a seat. I sat very still, dazed. The thump . . . thump . . . thump of the copter blades terrified me. Fear trickled down my spine. It suddenly hit me: it was the same noise from my room.

CHAPTER 8

THE CHANGELING

I couldn't see the face of the hooded figure in my dream, just his back as he crept away from me. No matter how fast I ran or how loud I screamed, I couldn't save Paul from falling. I woke up drenched in sweat and couldn't fall asleep for a long time. After that, Paul and the hooded figure were in my dreams every night, but I could never save him from falling off the cliff.

Each night, a sense of creepiness came over me. I trudged up the stairs dreading sleep, hugging myself under my quilt, curled into a ball. My mind was full of images: Paul, the shell, and other things I couldn't make sense of. Nothing seemed clear at first, but it became evident that I had to do something to save Paul.

Over a month had gone by, and Paul was still in a coma. I sat with him at the hospital each day so he wouldn't be alone while his mom worked. A ventilator kept him alive. I thought Paul would die—but what if he lived? Then what? Would he be a vegetable? I was scared.

Eventually, I realized what I had to do to save Paul. I made a pact with the devil—the thing inside the shell. I woke early one morning and dressed in a hurry, pulling on my jeans, and smoothing the wrinkles out of a top I didn't have time to iron.

In the kitchen, I made a bowl of cereal and ate it without tasting the food. Nana had errands to run and offered to drop me at the hospital. She came into the kitchen as I cleaned up my breakfast dishes.

"Are you ready, Skye? I have a dentist's appointment at nine o'clock."

"Let me run upstairs and brush my teeth. I'll meet you in the driveway."

When I got in the car, I tucked my red pack on the floor between my legs, and tears flooded my eyes.

Nana looked over at me. "Skye, what's wrong? Why are you crying?"

"All the people I love and care about are dying."

Nana shook her head. "Do you think you're jinxed? Don't be ridiculous, Skye."

Tears ran down my cheeks. "Paul is going to die. I can't handle someone else close to me dying again."

Nana took a deep breath. "You're doing all you can for him. Even though he's unconscious, I'm sure he knows you're there. Give it time, dear."

I leaned over and kissed her cheek. "I wish I were as strong as you. Nothing ever beats you down."

Nana put the van in gear and got on the road. "I'm not that strong. Life has thrown me a lot of curves. But the older you get, the more you learn to roll with the punches." She glanced over at me. "I'll cancel my appointment and come and sit with you and Paul."

My hand flew to my throat, and I sucked in a breath. "That's all right. I feel like being alone with him today. You go and run your errands." I couldn't let her interfere with my plan.

She pulled up in front of the hospital, and I got out. Gray clouds blanketed the sky, and the wind had turned cold.

Inside the lobby, I passed through the foyer into a corridor with signs mapping the various departments. An elevator took me to the second floor, where two tall glass doors were marked "ICU." I pushed the intercom button on the wall. The doors swung open, and the smell of disinfectant hit me as I walked down the corridor.

Patient cubicles with hanging curtains and glass walls surrounded the unit in a circle. Behind the nurse's station was a bank of monitors and equipment. One of the nurses waved at me, but I was too focused on the path to Paul's room to stop and talk.

As I stood in the doorway, my heart was pounding. Paul's head was elevated, wires ran out of his chest, and IV lines stuck out of his arm. A respirator hose was taped to his mouth. His cuts and bruises had healed since the accident, and despite all the equipment attached to his body, he looked peaceful.

I peered through the glass partition to see if anyone was paying attention to me. A stocky red-haired nurse looked up from behind the nurse's station. My heart skipped a beat, and I stepped back out of sight, giving him time to return to his duties. The chime of a bell signaled the nurse, and he headed down the hall.

It was now or never. I drew the drapes around Paul's bed. I wanted to run out of the room, but I had to be brave. I unzipped the red pack and pulled out the seashell. It throbbed warmly in my damp palm. My fingers parted the drawn curtain, and I peered out one more time to make sure no one was coming.

My fingers brushed Paul's cold cheek, and I held the conch to Paul's ear. "My dad told me that you could hear the ocean if you held a seashell to your ear," I whispered. "Listen to the shell, Paul. I want you to come back . . . Paul . . . please come back." I wept as I cradled the shell against his ear.

I leaned down, inhaling his earthy, masculine scent, and kissed his forehead as I curled my hand tightly around the shell. Paul's chest rose and fell in a steady rhythm. Ever since I'd found the shell, this had been my destiny. The dreams of being in a dark place weren't about Dad. Paul was in that place, and I had the means to save him. Tears streamed down my cheek. I wasn't going to let anyone else I loved die.

Suddenly, the shell pulsated, and a blast of energy knocked me on my butt. What had happened? What could have made it do that?

Stunned, I stood back up, with the shell clutched in my palm. Strangely, it felt lighter than before. I raised it up and down, balancing it in my hand, wondering if it was just my imagination. Was I losing it? Maybe I was going crazy.

All of a sudden, Paul's hand shot out and locked my wrist in a firm hold. I pulled back, twisting away, but I couldn't get loose. I stifled a scream.

I looked down at the bed. Paul's eyes were open. Oh, my God—his eyes were open! He raised his chin and studied me with brilliant blue eyes. But—his eyes were brown!

I stood there frozen, locked in his grip for breathless moments, his cobalt blue eyes staring at me while my mind denied what I was seeing.

Oh, God. What had I done?

CHAPTER 9

ROAD TO RECOVERY

After another six weeks, Paul was finally released home from rehab with physical and speech therapy visits twice a week, which was all the insurance would cover. The doctors claimed his eye color had changed due to the trauma he suffered from the fall. I went online. After much research, I couldn't find anything specific; it was anyone's guess.

During Paul's therapy and his recovery at home, I'd been there to help him, because Carolyn had to work, and Jeff had school. So instead of looking for a job, I stayed with Paul. I promised myself that I would take whatever steps were necessary to see that Paul, or whatever he was, recovered to the best of his ability.

Paul had to use a wheelchair because he was still too weak to walk. While he was in rehab, I took a caregiver class at the hospital. They taught me how to assist with Paul's needs so that I could participate in his recovery.

Nana was worried that I spent too much time caring for Paul; that it was becoming an obsession. The remorse and guilt of what I'd done to Paul seeped into my mind as the days and weeks passed. Nana was right; my whole world revolved around helping Paul, making me an emotional prisoner.

Paul couldn't eat solid food, so everything I spoon-fed him had to be put through the blender. I'd place a towel across his chest because he had trouble swallowing, and food dribbled down his chin. I also had to help him to get on and off the toilet. Plus he had a urinal on his nightstand. Usually, he could manage alone, but he had a habit of spilling the contents.

I also helped with his bathing. First, I transferred him to a bath chair in the walk-in shower. We did this twice a week, with sponge baths in between. The first time I had to undress Paul, a wave of embarrassment overcame me seeing him naked. His muscle tone and weight remained about the same as before the accident. But my discomfort quickly turned to sadness, seeing this once active young man reduced to an invalid.

I'd pull several bath wipes from the container and start washing under his arms and back. Next, I'd move down his chest and stomach to his groin. Even though I did this unconsciously, my hand tensed whenever I touched this part of his body. It was probably hormones causing my discomfort. My eyes would turn to his as I scrubbed, looking for a reaction, but his blank stare showed me he was unresponsive to my touch.

Afterward, I dressed Paul and sat him up in the wheelchair. Even though he couldn't speak, his eyebrows rose and fell whenever I spoke to him. As the days passed, I began to sense a strength in Paul and was no longer sure he was as helpless as he looked.

In the weeks that followed, his blue eyes didn't seem as vacant. It was like an undercurrent of energy sizzling behind them as he watched me. His direct stare made me uncomfortable. I was beginning to see him less and less as an invalid.

Day by day, Paul was getting stronger. But perhaps because I saw him so much, his recovery seemed slow. Finally, I started taking him outside for short walks in the wheelchair. It was too awkward to push him through the sand, but we could go around the block.

Next, Paul graduated to using a walker. Even though his legs were improving, his speech wasn't. He'd form a word or two with his lips, but they were slurred and hard to understand.

It wasn't long before Paul could walk short distances in the sand without the walker. One afternoon, he and I took a short walk on the beach. When we got to the shoreline, he stumbled and fell into the sand. Reaching out, I grasped his hands and pulled him up, but he toppled and crashed into me. We fell into the sand, his body on top, pressing against me. He smelled fresh, like powder—not like before the accident. I thought it must have been from all the wipes and lotion. Paul reached out his hand for mine, and I took it. He gave my fingers a gentle squeeze. I squeezed back, and he smiled.

I pushed Paul off and rolled onto my back, letting the sun warm my face. A gentle breeze blew across Paul's body, and I got another whiff of his clean scent. I sat up, rested my chin on my knees, and watched Paul bask in the sun. Even with his eyes closed, he looked too beautiful to be real. I studied his features, the strong chin, the chiseled nose.

Unable to help myself, I brushed my finger across his cheek, marveling at the perfect texture of his soft skin. His eyes opened, and the hint of a smile played on his lips. I leaned in and traced the outline of his mouth with my nail.

What was I doing? This wasn't the same Paul. I pulled my hand back, wondering if I was under some kind of spell.

I smoothed my hair back, trying to compose myself. "Paul, let's stand up."

I stood and tugged at him, keeping a firm stance in the sand. He glanced up at me with his dark lashes and blue eyes, and my knees went weak. He popped up and wobbled, and I leaned against him so he wouldn't topple. We stood, and I looked again into his deep blue eyes. So beautiful. I struggled to shake off my feelings. I had to concentrate on getting him back to normal.

"Afraid?" he said.

"No, of course not." I laughed, but the sound was fake.

His eyes stared at me without emotion. It made me feel on edge. I wondered if the thing inside of Paul was bad. I wondered why I wasn't scared of him. "You're not bad," I whispered. "No, I don't believe you're evil."

The seconds passed. His deep blue eyes held mine—until I finally looked away.

We walked back to his house, arm in arm. I wondered what was going through his jumbled mind.

He stopped, put his arms around me, and pressed his face against my hair. I pulled back, and he lifted my chin, examining my face. Then, something, a dream, struggled to break into my consciousness, and I felt myself drifting. I became hypnotized, immersed in the beauty of his blue eyes, and his words floated into my mind . . .

You heard my telepathic pleas to put the shell to the boy's ear. My entity is in this mind, and my DNA links with the body. I have a host. Any thoughts that remain concealed in his unconscious brain will be absorbed. I must learn your ideas, habits, and language to exist in this world and not draw attention to myself.

What I cannot assimilate from the broken mind of this being, I must learn from you. You had an emotional bond to this being and my entity while I occupied the shell.

You have given me a chance to live and interact with others. I feel your touch on this body. It overwhelms and exhilarates me.

A jolt ran through my body. I pulled back, dazed. My mind struggled against what I'd just perceived from his mind and the fog in my brain. Finally, I forced my eyes open. Paul studied me with an unsettling intelligence in his eyes that was so much different than his recent empty stare.

My pulse quickened as emotion and doubt rushed through me. Finally, I broke from his arms and backed away, wondering—had he been aware the whole time?

CHAPTER 10

REVELATION

That night, exhausted from the emotional stress of what had happened with Paul on the beach, I drifted off to sleep. My eyes opened to moonlight trickling through the window, illuminating the room. The clock glowed 2:15. The wind had blown the framed picture of Paul and me off the dresser. I got out of bed to set it back on the chest. When I went to shut the window, I thought I saw Paul out on the shore, lit by the moonlight. Then, he wandered into the surf. I wondered how he'd gotten out there without help. What if he was in trouble?

I turned on the lamp, threw on shorts and a shirt, and searched the nightstand for a flashlight. Then, slipping into the hall, I crept downstairs, avoiding the bottom stair that creaked so I wouldn't wake Nana. Outside, a gust of wind made me shiver. I ran across the damp sand toward the shore, to where I'd seen Paul from the window.

A pair of shorts and a t-shirt lying in the sand stopped me short. The full moon moved from behind a cloud, and

I froze. Paul stood in the water, naked. The moonlight silhouetted his broad shoulders and dark hair.

I turned away, confused. It wasn't like I hadn't seen him without clothes. Modesty takes a backseat when someone is helpless. His miraculous recovery frightened me more than seeing him in the ocean naked. I inched closer.

Suddenly, he spun around and gazed at me with his deep blue eyes. "I summoned you, and here you are." His voice was distinct and articulate.

"Paul, you can speak?" I sputtered. "What are you doing out here? How come you're naked? What's going on?"

"The ocean beckons me and gives me strength. The shell held me captive for so long that I desire to be free of constrictions."

"Paul, something is inside your mind. I put it there when you were in the coma. It came from the shell. It's making you act crazy."

"I am not the human, Paul. In this mind, his presence is weak. I am able to extract images and concepts from the remnants of his existence. Words develop gradually from this damaged brain. That is how I speak."

I drew back and studied his face. It was the same handsome face but less human—rigid and unemotional. But then, Paul had been through so much in the past few months.

"Had you not relocated my entity in this body, it would not have survived."

Tears filled my eyes, and I clenched my hands. "I don't know how to feel about what I did to you, but I couldn't let Paul die." I raised my head and looked into his stunning blue eyes. "Will you remain in his body forever?"

Paul remained steady as the waves tumbled over his hips that swayed with the rhythm of the tide. His eyes flashed cobalt blue. "Should I leave this body, it will die."

"Then, there's no hope. Paul will never return." Tears blurred my vision. I hadn't saved Paul—I'd saved only his body for this creature to possess. Ironically, this creature had moved out of one shell and into another.

Discouraged, I wanted to leave. But there were so many unanswered questions that I had to stay. I moved closer to the shoreline, to the thing that Paul had become. The rolling surf soaked my flip-flops. A breeze blew across my face, and the soft scent of powder assaulted my senses. I leaned in and inhaled, overwhelmed by a tingling sensation rushing throughout my body. I shuddered. Our eyes locked, and I faltered. Something about his presence made me weak. I held his gaze, struggling to read his thoughts.

Brushing my damp palms against my shorts, I swallowed without breaking eye contact. "Yesterday, you couldn't walk without help. Your speech was irrational. Suddenly, in one day, you make a miraculous recovery. What happened?"

"This body required time to regenerate. Fragments of this human's mind and your thoughts aided me in understanding your language."

I stepped forward, clenching my fingers into a fist. "You read my mind?"

He leaned back and crossed his arms. His eyes bore into mine. "I use telepathy to interact while you are asleep. I cannot comprehend your thoughts when your mind is awake and active."

The constant roar of the surf was suddenly louder. The waves lapped my legs. I inched closer, raising my voice. "Let's get this straight. You can't read my mind, but you can communicate with me through telepathy? Isn't that reading my mind?"

He lifted an eyebrow, and the trace of a smile crossed his face. It was Paul, before the accident, before the entity. My heart skipped a beat. "Do you have a name?"

His eyes glittered aquamarine. "Not in a sense you would understand. On my world, we interacted with our minds through telepathy."

"I'd like to call you by another name. We can make one up."

"Call me Paul. To anyone that knew Paul, I am this human. Should anyone discover that I am from another planet, they will lock me away—a specimen to examine. Humanity would consider me an adversary."

"How about we find a doctor . . . scientist . . . or someone else who can help you? Someone who can find a way to restore Paul?"

His lip curled back over his teeth, and his blue eyes blazed sapphire. "It would place me in danger."

A horrible thought suddenly crossed my mind. "Did you have anything to do with Paul falling off the cliff?"

His hands clenched into fists. "I'm an opportunist, not a killer."

At that moment, I decided his name would be Alien Paul. He was an intruder, an impostor. He didn't deserve Paul's name. The surf pounded my ankles as we gazed into each other's eyes. His eyes cooled to turquoise; they were striking against the background of his bronzed skin and dark hair. I had to gather my thoughts and choose my words carefully so I wouldn't upset him.

"If you don't seek help . . . go to a doctor . . . then there is no hope for Paul." Tears ran down my cheeks.

He studied my face. "I perceive you are upset. Nothing I can do will bring back the Paul you knew. You must reveal nothing about my origins."

"Who would listen to me, anyway? They would think I was crazy. You talked about being locked up and examined. Can you imagine what would happen if I spread around town that you're an alien from another planet? I don't think you have anything to worry about."

With a sense of hopelessness, I turned and sloshed through the surf. Sand stuck to my wet flip-flops as I headed back to the cottage. I went at a steady pace and didn't look back. I had unleashed this alien, a taker of souls. My actions had saved Paul's life, but at what cost? I trudged through the sand, my wet sandals as heavy as the guilt in my mind. I made this mess. It was my responsibility to own up to whatever happened with Alien Paul.

CHAPTER 11

THE NAKED TRUTH

All the lights were out at the house, meaning Nana was still asleep. I tiptoed upstairs and climbed into bed, intending to tell Nana about my encounter with Paul in the morning. Then she'd be able to counsel me on what to do. My mind raced, thinking about Alien Paul. I finally sank into an exhausted, dreamless sleep in the early morning hours.

The sun beating through the window on my face woke me. I perched on the side of the bed, dizzy and confused. The hot water in the shower didn't last as long as I wanted, but long enough to clear my head. Last night, I'd thought confiding in Nana was a good idea. But after some consideration, I wasn't so sure. I wouldn't lie to her, but I wouldn't drop everything in her lap at once. At least not the alien part, not yet. I want to see what Alien Paul would do. Even though Nana had an open mind, she might think I'd lost mine if I told her about the entity. It was my problem, so I had to suck it up and find out more about Alien Paul's intentions.

Outside, I stood by the door of the potting shed. A collection of gardening tools and equipment hung from hooks on the wall. A stream of sunlight shining through a milky cobweb-covered window lit up the narrow worktable where Nana was working in her baggy lavender t-shirt, blue jeans, and pink garden crocs. Clumps of dirt clung to the strands of silver hair from a ponytail that had come loose from her rainbow scrunchie as she packed clay pots with soil. Just then, she sensed my presence and paused, peering up at me.

"Oh, Skye, how long have you been there?" Her fingers brushed at the clods of dirt at the ends of her hair.

"Not long. I didn't want to disturb you."

"You're never a bother. What's on your mind?"

"I need to talk to you about something when you have time."

"Let's go sit on the deck. I could use a break." Nana came over and took my hand.

We moved to the deck and sat at the weather-beaten picnic table across from each other. I gazed at the ocean, wondering where to start.

"What's wrong? You look upset."

I drew a breath and let it out. "Last night, I woke up and looked out the window. The full moon lit the beach. Someone that looked like Paul was out in the surf. I got dressed and went to see if he needed help."

"You shouldn't be out on the beach in the dark. What if it was a stranger? He might have attacked you. This worries me, honey."

"I didn't approach him until I was certain it was Paul. Here's the strangest part. Paul was in the water, and his speech was normal when he spoke. And he could walk without help."

Nana rubbed her brow and combed her fingers through her hair, scattering bits of potting soil across the table. "You mean he made a complete recovery?"

"Yes, but Paul was different. His speech was robotic, not normal, like how he used to talk. I know it sounds crazy, but how could he recover that fast in a day?"

Nana's eyes narrowed. "Oh, honey, are you certain it wasn't a dream?"

I studied Nana's kind face, every line, every crease. I loved her so much. Finally, I choked out, "I'm . . . I'm positive it was real."

Nana's intelligent hazel eyes gazed into mine as she sat across the table. The silence made me nervous. My fingers drummed the tabletop, and I looked away.

"Did you leave anything out . . . something you're not telling me?"

My stomach churned, and sweat broke out on my forehead. Nana knew I was hiding something. I'd always been a bad liar. I broke eye contact and gazed out at the beach. Finally, I turned back, met her eyes, and swallowed. "Oh, my God, Nana. Paul was in the water naked." It was all I could think to say without spilling the whole truth.

Nana leaned across the table, her eyebrows lifted, and the hint of a smile crossed her lips. "Naked?"

"Nothing happened." I pressed my lips together and held her gaze, showing her I was serious.

Nana leaned back and chuckled. "I was your age once. It was 1967, the Summer of Love. They called us hippies, flower children. We fought the establishment and protested the Vietnam War. I wasn't ashamed to shed my clothes. We enter this world naked and leave the same way. There is nothing wrong with nudity as long as you only give your body freely to the one you love."

Wow. That had been easier than I'd expected. "Thanks for understanding, Nana."

Her brow wrinkled, and her face turned serious. "Now, what about Paul and his change of condition?"

"I'm going to go to his house and talk to his mom and brother. See what they know about his speedy recovery."

Nana came over and rubbed my shoulder. "Want me to come along?"

"Thanks, but I can handle it. Why don't you finish what you were doing in the shed? I'll fill you in on what I find out when I get back."

"Take the van, honey. And don't forget, I'm right here if you need me." Nana smiled and gave me a thumbs-up.

Tears flooded my eyes, and I ran over and threw my arms around her soft, round body. "I love you, Nana." Hugging her tighter, I whispered, "We'll talk when I get back." Then, with a heavy heart, I released my hold on her, grabbed the car keys from under the cabinet, and headed out the door.

CHAPTER 12

COMING TO TERMS

On the drive over to Paul's house, I thought about Nana. I shouldn't have laid all my problems on her. She was getting older, and I needed to learn to cope without involving her. I was getting better at driving the old VW bus. I only ground the gears twice on the way over.

As I pulled into the driveway, the front door flew open. Paul's brother, Jeff, ran outside. The spikes of his sun-bleached auburn hair stood up on his head; his expression was troubled. His t-shirt and shorts were messy, like he'd slept in them. Something was wrong.

"I'm glad you're here," he said.

"Jeff, what's going on?"

"Paul is acting strange."

"Strange, how?"

"Let's go inside. I'll show you." Jeff ran ahead of me and opened the front door. We walked across the spacious living room. Large cathedral windows overlooked the beach. This home was so much larger and newer than Nana's little cottage.

"Jeff, I came by to ask you and your mom if you have noticed anything different or unusual about Paul since yesterday."

"Are you kidding? He's been acting weird since he got out of the hospital," Jeff said.

"But has he improved? The way he walks, his speech?"

Jeff grabbed my hand and pulled me down the hall. We stopped in front of Paul's room. Jeff pushed the door open. "Have a look for yourself."

Paul stood with his back to me, looking out the window. He lifted one leg, then the other, like he was exercising. I wanted to ask him what he was doing, but I stopped myself.

Jeff scooted forward. "He hasn't been able to move like that since before the accident. His speech is different—not Paul. He's not my brother."

"What does your mom say about it?"

He sniffed. "She said that since Paul has a traumatic brain injury, he might never be the same." Tears spilled from his eyes.

I touched his shoulder. "At least he's getting better." It was all I could think to say.

Jeff wiped his nose on the back of his hand. "He was all I had since Dad left. Now, he hardly pays attention to me."

"We have to be patient with him. But your mom's right, he has a long way to go, and it won't be easy."

Paul didn't acknowledge that we were in the room. Instead, he kept doing the same stretches while gazing out the window. I was worried, but I didn't want to alarm Jeff.

"I'm going to talk to Paul alone for a while."

"Good luck with that," Jeff snorted. He turned and stormed down the hall.

I shut the door, moved behind Paul, and put my hand on his shoulder. "Paul?" He cocked his head and turned his ear toward my voice. That was when I noticed that he had his shirt on backward. If this were the old Paul, I would have laughed. But this was an imposter. I burst into tears.

I wiped my wet eyes with the back of my hands and dried them on my shorts. Then, I took Paul's hand and led him to the bed. "Sit down; I want to talk to you."

He turned, bent his knees, and lowered his butt to the mattress like a stiff robot. The fire in his eyes from the night before was gone. They were still that beautiful shade of blue but tired, weary. I sat beside him and curled my hair back behind my ears.

I took a deep breath. "Last night, you were animated—alive. You're sluggish today—mechanical. What's changed?"

He looked straight ahead like his mind was processing my words. I smoothed the wrinkles out of my shorts and tugged at my shirt. His head turned in my direction.

"The sea has been my home since I arrived on this world. I draw energy from the ocean. The dynamics and movement of the tides rejuvenate this body and mind."

His speech was slow, enunciating every word. Not like last night—no longer Neptune, king of the sea, the warrior who knew no bounds.

Something tugged at my heart. This alien from another world was lost. There was no way I could abandon him.

I stood and faced him. "Lift your arms."

He raised them. I reached down, pulled off his shirt, and slid it back over his head the right way.

"Oh, Paul, what happened? Last night you were strong and confident in the surf. Now you can barely move. I don't understand?"

He slowly lifted his chin, examining my face with his faded eyes. "Meet me on the beach tonight. I must speak to you."

"Paul, or whoever you are, I need some answers."

"Meet me at eleven, and I will explain. The place we met last night. You must reveal nothing of this. Come alone."

"OK, I'll meet you tonight," I bent down, kissed his forehead, and strolled out of the room, leaving him sitting on the bed.

I ran into Paul's mom in the living room on my way out. She was pacing back and forth, talking on her cell with a client. She held up one finger, signaling me to wait. I sank into the brown leather couch, waiting for her to finish. Carolyn Lucerno was a class act. She worked in real estate, pitching dreams of seaside homes. Her cuffed khaki pants, light blue dressy tee, and black blazer hung perfectly on her slight frame. Not an ounce of fat on Carolyn; she wouldn't allow it.

Carolyn ended her call, perched next to me on the couch, and grabbed my hand. "Skye, isn't it exciting? Paul's making such great progress."

"He's looking better." I was at a loss for words.

Carolyn brushed a lock of highlighted auburn hair from her forehead. "I'm excited that he has made so much progress in the last twenty-four hours." She squeezed my hand. "I have a feeling he'll be back to his old self in no time."

I sat there speechless, hoping she didn't notice the sweat on my forehead or my clammy palms. I wondered what she would say if she knew the truth, that her son was an alien. Finally, she let go of my hand, and it dropped into my lap.

Carolyn's wide eyes blinked, and she smiled. "I owe a lot of his recovery to you, Skye. If it weren't for you, I would have had to hire home health nurses—strange people coming and going with no one to oversee them. If there's anything I can do for you, just name it."

"Helping Paul has given me a purpose and takes my mind off the loss of my parents," I pushed my palms into the soft leather of the sofa and scooted forward. "I'd better go. Nana's expecting me."

We stood. Carolyn looked into my eyes and squeezed my shoulder. "Some people say I'm cold. Sometimes, you've got to be a bitch to get by, especially if you're a single mother. But, to me, you're family. I know you have your Nana, but you also have us."

I nodded. "Thanks," I said as I bolted for the front door, so she wouldn't see the tears flooding my eyes.

Back at the cottage, the aroma of chicken from the crockpot filled the house. Nana sat on the couch, unlacing her Nikes. "I just got back from a walk on the beach. I ran into a nice-looking man around my age. He tried to strike up a conversation, but his speedo ruined the moment," she chuckled. "My feet are on fire. Trudging through the sand in sneakers isn't easy."

I laughed. "Oh my God, Nana, TMI."

Nana's eyes narrowed. "What did you find out over at Paul's?"

"I spoke to his mom. She's happy that his condition is improving. I only wish I could do more to help him."

"No one has done more for Paul. You have worked hard helping with his rehabilitation," Nana said.

"I thought I could help him, but he's not the same as before."

"He may never be the same. Accept him the way he is now. At least he's showing improvement."

I sank into the armchair, took a deep breath, and blew it out. "Last night on the beach, he was strong, powerful. Today, the exact opposite—he was sluggish."

I was tired of lying and wanted to tell Nana about what was really going on with Paul, but I held back. Tears filled my eyes. Nana went to the table and plucked a tissue from the box.

"He's had a traumatic brain injury," she said, handing it to me. "He's confused and apt to say or do anything."

"Oh, Nana, I want him back the way he was before the accident."

"It might not be possible, but time will tell." Nana came over, opened her arms, and gave me a big hug.

I pulled back and studied her face. "Nana, you know about so many strange things. What do you think stardust smells like?" I needed to know her answer.

Nana's brows lifted. "You mean debris from exploding stars? I'm not certain, but likely pure uncontaminated dust or powder. The power generated by a nova would revert atoms to their basic structure, at least from everything I've read. Why do you ask?"

Paul smells like powder.

I changed the subject. "The chicken's making my mouth water. When are we going to eat?"

I followed Nana into the kitchen. She lifted the lid on the crockpot. "It should be ready in about an hour."

It wasn't long before we were sitting at the table, eating. Nana made tender baby new potatoes and sweet corn to go with the chicken. As always, everything was delicious. As we silently ate, I was thankful that Nana didn't ask me any more questions.

After dinner, I helped with the dishes and watched the news. I told Nana I was tired and went up to my room. I'd hoped that she would, too. At quarter after ten, my damp palm twisted the doorknob, and I peered out my door. All the lights were out.

I snuck out of the house at a little before eleven. I brought a flashlight and hiked down to the water to find Paul. When I reached the shoreline, he was nowhere in sight. The damp sea air made the minutes seem like hours. Finally, a lone figure moved down the beach. I could tell it was Paul by the long strides crunching in the sand. He wore jeans and a hoodie. The moonlight lit his face as he strolled up to me. I stared into his deep blue eyes. He smiled, and my heart beat faster. Maybe I shouldn't have come.

I balled my hand into a fist and rubbed it against my thigh, resisting the urge to reach out and stroke his cheek. Instead, I stammered, "You're late."

"I had to establish the family unit was asleep."

I bit my lip. "Paul, what's going on?"

"I need you to help me adapt to this world." His eyes bored into mine. "You rescued me from the shell and delivered me into this consciousness."

"You already control Paul, so why do you need me?"

"Just his body. His emotions, his desires, and his memories remain shrouded."

A lump formed in my throat. "Paul's alive?"

"Only remnants of his prior awareness."

"Oh, I see," I whispered, so my voice wouldn't break.

Sensing my anguish, Alien Paul brushed my cheek. "I need you. You understand me—you know what I am."

I stumbled backward, and he reached out and caught my arm. A jolt of electricity ran through my body. I shivered and pulled away from his grasp.

It took me a moment to remember where I was. "You came from the shell. Of that, I'm certain, but I don't know what you are."

"My entity traveled from a planet many light years away through a spiral vortex that transported us to this world."

"I'm lost. How did you travel here? What happened to your body?"

"We shed our bodies, and our entities remained. You call it a soul. We traveled through a wormhole, a rift in space and time, and arrived inside seashells in this ocean. The shells contain a logarithmic spiral, a portal from which we could exit. The saline and pH component of the sea was equal to our environment, and we thrived."

"You traveled here with others? Where are they?"

"They fled the sea and migrated into human bodies. Being buried under the ocean caused my connection with the others to dim over time."

"You stayed in the shell? Why didn't you join the others?

"An earthquake sent my shell into an abyss, sealed under tons of silt. Another recent quake caused a rift in the ocean floor, which discharged the shell into the tides. Finally, it washed up in the shallows where you found it." Alien Paul held my gaze with his gorgeous blue eyes.

His stare made my knees weak. "Why did you come here?"

"In search of the Bahlari."

"What is that?"

"They are a race of aliens whose purpose is to invade civilizations like Earth and cause chaos and destruction."

I brushed my hair back from my face and looked around. "Are they still here? The Bahlari?"

"Yes. That is why I need your assistance to adapt to this world. I must hunt down the Bahlari and rid this world of their malevolent influence on humanity."

He stared unblinking with those intolerable blue eyes. I wanted to cling to his broad, muscular chest and tell him I'd help him. That everything was going to be OK.

Instead I said, "I'm going to have to think this through. I want to help you, but I'm not sure to what extent. I've got to go now." I pulled away and headed home without looking back.

On the way home, I realized that I already knew the answer to his question. I didn't know if there was ever a choice, not after putting that thing into Paul's head—I was in too deep. It was my fault for what I'd done to change him. It was too late to undo it. What Paul had become was because of me. I accepted that and was willing to take responsibility for my actions.

But other than all that—when I thought of Alien Paul, his extraterrestrial robotic voice, his hypnotic eyes, and his sensual presence—all I wanted was to be with him.

CHAPTER 13

WHITE LIES

That night, I tossed and turned, waking often. Alien Paul invaded my dreams. However, my perception of him had changed. These dreams were different, sensual. When the sun rose, I was tired but also tense. I showered, pulled on a green tank top and black shorts, and headed downstairs.

Nana sat at the table by the bay window that looked out to the beach, sipping her coffee. She wore a colorful blouse, bright yellow with big black circles. Her loose silver hair curled around her rosy cheeks, lit by the sunlight streaming into the kitchen. I thought back to Nana's pictures of herself from years earlier—of the attractive blonde girl in cut-off Daisy Duke shorts with long shapely legs. After all those years, she was still a handsome woman. I filled my mug with coffee and sat at the table.

"You look tired. Didn't you sleep well?" she asked.

I rubbed my eyes. "Not really. In my dreams, my mind was traveling a thousand miles an hour, the usual stuff."

She raised an eyebrow. "You have been through so much lately. It's only natural that you have dreams and can't sleep. It should be easier now that Paul is on the road to recovery. Nice to hear that he's getting around again."

I took a sip of coffee and brushed my hair back. "It might be because of me that Paul is acting this way."

"Of course, it's because of you. You have helped with his therapy and encouraged him to fight this battle. You're the reason he's improving."

I bit my lip. This wasn't going well. Time to try another strategy. "Nana, do you believe in aliens from other planets?"

Nana leaned back and smiled. "I lived through the Age of Aquarius. Back then, we were waiting for the Mother Ship to drop out of the sky and rescue us from Vietnam and all the other crazy stuff going on in the world. Of course, I believe in aliens. It's a fact that there are more stars in the universe than grains of sand on all the beaches on Earth. It would be unfathomable to think that we are alone in this universe with all those stars and planets out there. So why do you ask?"

I sipped my coffee and watched her over the rim of my cup. "Sometimes—I dream about aliens." I fidgeted in my seat.

Nana studied my face. "Is that why you're not sleeping at night?"

My tongue traced my lower lip. Where should I start? Should I give her bits and pieces or let it all out at once? It sounded like she could handle it—and be objective.

I drew a breath and blew it out. "Remember the big conch shell that I found on the beach?"

Nana nodded. "It was strange that you found that shell in the surf. Conch shells are native to the Gulf of Mexico and the Caribbean. It was one of the most beautiful shells I've ever seen on this beach. I wonder how it got there."

"Something inside the shell spoke to me in my dreams." I leaned forward. "I'm not crazy. It happened."

Nana lifted her mug, took a sip, and set it down. "What did it say?"

"That it came from another planet and was buried under the sea. When it finally washed up on shore, I found it and brought it home. At first, I thought the voice was Dad's, but I eventually realized it wasn't him. The voice was alien, distant, and cold. Not like Dad at all." I swallowed and rubbed my damp palms against my shorts.

Nana stood, refilled her cup, then returned to the table and sat down. "Why didn't you throw it back in the sea? You didn't have to keep it."

I shook my head. "I was curious. It fascinated me. I looked forward to communicating with this entity from another world. It was special."

Nana cocked her head. "Is it still interacting with you?"

"Not since I took it to Paul in the hospital."

"You took the shell to the hospital?" Nana said.

"Paul wasn't going to pull through. He was going to die. I needed to do something. The seashell was my last chance to try and save him."

Nana stood and put her hands on her generous hips. "What in the world would make you think that this shell could help Paul?"

"A strange feeling made me think that the shell could save Paul. So I put it up close to his ear, hoping he could hear the voice inside. Then, he woke up. But his eyes were blue. And he wasn't the same," I sobbed.

Nana reached for a tissue and handed it to me. "It's OK, dear. It was a coincidence. When you put the shell to his ear, he just happened to come out of the coma. You're reading too much into this."

I got up and took my cup over to the sink. I turned on the faucet and shook my head. "No, Nana. It wasn't my imagination. There was something alien inside of that shell. And now it's inside of Paul." I pushed the hair out of my eyes, dumped dish soap on the sponge, and concentrated on scrubbing my mug, avoiding Nana's gaze.

·· 🐚 ··

CHAPTER 14

WHERE THE WATER ENDS

The following day at the breakfast table, I scraped the remnants of scrambled eggs and peach salsa off my plate, along with the last bits of sourdough toast slathered with Nana's homemade strawberry jam. She planned on rearranging the potting shed after breakfast. When I told her I was going swimming, she warned me that there was a storm out in the Pacific and the waves were higher than usual.

On the beach, eight-foot waves crashed against the shoreline. I was a good swimmer, so I wasn't afraid. I took off barefoot across the sand in my black one-piece. The sun warmed my back, and the wind beat against my face. The energy of the sea invigorated me. The towering waves rolled onto the shore and retreated, digging the sand out from beneath my feet. I shivered, but a warm ripple washed the chill away. The wind whipped at my hair, carrying the aroma of salt and kelp.

I moved out into the ocean as the waves struck my body. The water was cold, so I closed my eyes and arched my body to begin a shallow dive. I swam hard, turning from side to side, diving, and kicking, not realizing I was drifting farther and farther from shore.

When my eyes opened, the coastline was far away. The current had pulled me out to sea. I paddled and kicked, but the more I fought, the farther out I went. The few people on the shore looked like ants. I swam parallel to the riptide, as I knew to do, but I made no headway. The coastline grew smaller and smaller. I screamed for help, but my cries went unheard.

Exhausted, I floated on my back to save energy. Above, gulls flew and swooped through the air, making me wish I could grow wings and fly to shore.

I started to scream again, hoping someone would hear me, but no one did. The undertow pulled me farther out. I dove under the water to try and beat the current, but it made no difference. The constant tugging zapped my strength. I plunged under the water and popped up again and again, gasping for air. My leg cramped, and I shrieked in pain. I was sinking under the surf; my pulse pounded in my neck. My chest swelled. I needed air. Shimmers of sunlight danced above me. I needed to break the surface.

OK . . . OK . . . I'm strong. I can get through this.

But I was in too much agony to surface. So, this is drowning . . .

From a sky I thought I would never see again, rays of sunlight glittered through the water. As panic faded into numbness, my heartbeat slowed. The shimmering walls of water were beautiful. I was sinking; my lungs burned with a hunger for air. Water trickled down my throat. I curled up into a fetal ball and descended into the depths . . .

Daddy . . . Mommy, I'm so sorry . . . I'm coming . . . wait for me . . .

Ever so slowly, I sank into the dark, icy cold water. Everything was fading away. I didn't want to die like this, but it was too hard to fight, so I let the darkness blanket me.

Then, a strong arm seized me around the waist. My instinct was to fight, but I was yanked to the surface too fast. I broke water, gasping for breath . . . I whirled around . . .

"Paul!" I coughed—spitting water. My throat was on fire. How did he find me?

"Do not speak. You must regain your strength." His jaw was set, and his eyes glowed sapphire.

Suddenly, the riptide sucked me back under. Again, Paul pulled me to the surface. He wrapped his arms through my armpits in a tight embrace against his chest, rolled on his back, and started kicking. I stared up at the sky as we ripped through the waves. But something was wrong. We were going so fast, too fast. It wasn't normal. We shouldn't be going this fast. Although I was exhausted, adrenaline coursed through my body. Paul's breathing was steady as his muscular legs beat powerful kicks, and we reached the shore in no time.

He pulled me to my feet when we hit the shallows and dragged me from the water. I was cradled to his chest as we fell in a heap onto the sand. I raised my chin and studied his chiseled features—his deep blue eyes. "How did you do that? You must have superhuman strength."

He rippled his shoulders. "The ocean makes me powerful."

I reached out and traced his cheek with my fingertips. "You saved my life."

He put his hand on my waist. "I sensed you were in trouble. I will not let anything happen to you. You are important to me."

I slid my hand around his waist and turned into his arms.

He reached down and stroked my wet hair from the top of my head to my breast. His hand rested there on my rapidly beating heart. He cocked his head as if listening, and the trace of a smile lightened his face.

I slid my hand around his neck, pulling his face to mine. Our lips touched, and I tasted salt on his lips. He pulled back, then dipped down, and our lips met again. The tenderness of his kiss turned into a hunger. My heart was pounding with a desire—a need that sent a jolt through my body. A gust of wind blew, and Alien Paul's powdery scent reminded me that he wasn't human—wasn't Paul. I ran my hands down my forearms and shivered.

He lifted my chin and studied my face. "Is this being human?"

I shook my head, "For me? No. Not like this." I laughed, then stopped. It wasn't funny. I was falling for him, but I couldn't get it out of my mind that I was cheating on Paul.

Resting against his bare chest, I turned to him. "I'm eighteen, and Paul was also eighteen. I don't know how old you are, but I have a feeling you're much older."

"My entity was equal to your age when I came to this world. Inside the shell, time stopped."

There was so much more I wanted to ask. But I felt satisfied, just cradled in his arms. I turned my head and stared out over the vast ocean. A strange, unfamiliar sensation ran through me. I wanted to stay in his arms forever.

I should have died that day. Instead, I was resurrected.

CHAPTER 15

A NIGHT ON THE TOWN

The following day, Nana suggested I take Paul to dinner to celebrate his recovery. The harbor, on Friday nights, hosted a street fair. Most locals began their weekend with a night out at one of the restaurants on the pier.

At first, I nixed the idea; I didn't think Paul was ready for crowds. But after giving it some thought, I was excited to show Alien Paul a night on the town. I called Carolyn and ran it past her. She thought it was a great idea. I planned to pick Paul up at six that evening.

I decided to spring for an extravagant surf and turf dinner at The Golden Lobster. It was pricey, but I had money saved from Dad's insurance for my college fund. In addition, I had this fabulous dress I was dying to wear tucked in the back of the closet.

I showered, curled my hair, and applied a little makeup. My platform sandals matched my classic white lace cotton sundress. Fall was in the air, so I pulled out one of my hoodies.

Standing in front of the full-length mirror behind my bedroom door, I was nervous and giddy; it felt like prom night. I grabbed my purse and headed downstairs with my hoodie thrown over my shoulder.

Nana stood in the living room. "Skye, you look fabulous, but there is no way you're going to wear that sweatshirt."

"It's all I have, and the pier will get cold after the sun goes down."

"Wait, I have an idea." Nana turned, walked out of the room, and returned a few minutes later with a soft knitted wrap draped over her arm. It was the most beautiful spun colors of tans, grays, blues, and beiges I had ever seen.

"One of my friends went to Peru and brought this back for me as a gift. Isn't it gorgeous?" She tossed it to me.

I caught it and handed her the hoodie. "I'll trade you." I wrapped it around my shoulders, hugged her, and whispered, "I love you, Nana."

She squeezed me tighter. "You look lovely. I'm glad you're finally able to get out and have some fun. You deserve it. Have a good time. Any man would be proud to show you off."

Before pulling away, I kissed her cheek. "Thanks, I'm looking forward to it."

I went out to the garage and got in the van. Paul's house was only a mile away, but I didn't want to walk back in the dark. When I drove into the driveway, I had only ground the gears once. I was mastering the stick shift.

Carolyn greeted me at the door. "What a beautiful dress, Skye." She kissed my cheek.

Alien Paul came strolling down the hallway and stood next to me. He wore a pale blue Nike polo and khakis. His shirt brought out the blue in his eyes. He was so handsome; my legs went weak.

He looked at me with a crooked smile. "Are these appropriate clothes?"

I bit my lip to hide a smile. "Perfect, you look great." It touched my heart that he was worried about what I thought.

"You two have a good time tonight," Carolyn said. She squeezed Paul's shoulder and winked at me as she hustled us to the door.

We walked out to the van, and I expected him to open my door even though I was driving, but he went to the other side and got in. I started the engine, and we drove silently to the pier. The street was crowded with tourists and vehicles. I cruised up and down the side streets and spotted a parking space far from the dock.

It was dusk when we arrived at the entrance to the pier. Sparkly lights crisscrossed the boardwalk and swayed in the breeze. The twinkling lights in the shop windows reminded me of when Mom and Dad took me to Disneyland. A calm, salty breeze fluffed my hair. It was magical.

I took Paul's hand and leaned on his arm as we walked. His clean scent assaulted my senses. We passed a shop advertising locally grown fruits and vegetables. Baskets of strawberries, apples, and peaches lined the tables, along with tomatoes, zucchini, and a vast assortment of herbs.

Music played from somewhere in the distance. A breeze blew the aroma of fried fish and chips from a cafe down the way. My head swung side to side, taking it all in. The Golden Lobster was at the end of the pier, with a panoramic ocean view. We were early for our 7:00 pm reservation, so we sat outside and watched the tourists and boats in the harbor pass by.

The hostess never took her eyes off Paul in the crowded restaurant as she led us to a booth big enough for four, upholstered in red leather. "Thank you," I said as we sat.

She didn't acknowledge me but spoke to Paul. "Your server will be right out." He innocently smiled, and she backed away, knocking the salt and pepper shakers off the table. She bent down to pick them up and, on the way up, whacked her head on the table. Then, she made a hasty retreat to the kitchen.

I snickered. "It looks like your newfound strength isn't your only attribute."

He furrowed his brow; he seemed confused.

"Let's just say you have your way with more than just the waves." I could tell he didn't get what I was saying. "I mean, she's sexually attracted to you."

He smiled. "She wants to mate with me?"

I leaned forward. "You got it. You have a physical attraction about you. I can't figure out if it's your eyes, innocent ways, or your body odor."

He smiled wider and flashed his teeth. "Do you want to mate with me?"

The older couple in the next booth overheard him and looked over at me. I turned back to Paul, feeling the fire on my face. "Before all that, we're supposed to get to know each other, go on dates, then see where it leads," I said, barely above a whisper.

The server arrived and handled herself better than the hostess, but not by much. Her back was to me as she handed the menus to Paul.

"I'm Tiffany. Can I get you anything? Um, something to drink?"

Paul looked at me with a blank expression.

I tapped her on the shoulder and broke her spell. She turned around and speared me with a glare.

"I'll order for both of us." The way she threw me daggers, I was tempted to explain that it was his birthday. But then, I got mad. Was this what was going to happen every time we went out? If so, I'd need a bigger purse to carry the baseball bat.

"Can we have two Cokes?" I sounded like I was begging.

"I'll be right back." She abruptly turned away, but it didn't escape me that she flashed Paul another smile on her way to the kitchen.

We sat looking into each other's eyes. Alien Paul's face appeared relaxed, but his posture was stiff as he perched at the edge of his seat. I was concerned that he'd be overwhelmed in the bustling, crowded room. This was the first time he'd been out in public since he took over Paul's body.

I scooted forward in my seat. "What do you think about this place? I mean, coming here to eat?"

He raised an eyebrow. "Thoughts assault my mind, a hive of activity and noise. A cornucopia of smells and flavors."

I shook my head. "Where do you come up with those words? 'Cornucopia?' I know what it means, but normal people don't use it, except at Thanksgiving."

He frowned and pointed a finger at the older couple in the next booth. "Those humans think I am taking advantage of you."

The couple looked up from their meal, and I reached over and wrestled his hand down onto the table. "It's not polite to point," I scolded.

The server appeared with our Cokes and a warm breadbasket wrapped in a cloth napkin. As she passed a couple of plates across the table, she flashed Paul another smile. "Do you want to order?" she asked him. Tiffany's tip was getting smaller by the minute.

"Paul, what do you want to eat?" I blurted.

"I will consume what you eat," he answered.

"We'll both have the six-ounce sirloin and shrimp platter," I said to the server's backside.

She jotted down our order and left, but not without flashing another smile at Paul. Enough was enough. This was really starting to bother me. I pulled a slice of warm crusty bread off the mini loaf and slathered butter over it, then slid the basket over to Paul. He watched and followed my lead. He was good at paying attention to the details of human behavior. It wouldn't be long before he adapted. I took a bite of the soft, warm bread and looked across the table. Paul bit into the roll, lifted his head and smiled with sweet satisfaction. I melted like the butter on my bread.

Tiffany brought our crisp salads with slices of cool cucumber, tomatoes, and radish slivers. We had barely finished our salads when the sizzling sirloins came, well-marbled and medium-rare. The tasty butterfly shrimp was seared with garlic butter. Tiffany fluttered around the table like a moth around a porch light, trying to get Paul's attention. It was impossible to hold a decent conversation. We managed to get through the meal, and I paid the tab.

Outside, we walked arm in arm down the boardwalk, enjoying the cool ocean air and the twinkling lights. The crowd was thinning, and I was drowsy after all that heavenly food. So good, in fact, I ended up leaving Tiffany a twenty percent tip. I really couldn't blame her for falling for Alien Paul's charms.

A figure moved in the shadows just outside my vision. I turned, and yards off to my right was Karly. She must have been on her way home after closing the shop. She was the last person I wanted to run into tonight—too many bad memories. I never wanted to see her again.

I turned back to Paul, but he was gone. My eyes searched the pier. There he was—headed in Karly's direction. I took a deep breath and ran over to intercept him.

I took Paul's arm and tried to pull him back; he kept pushing forward. He was too strong for me, but I wouldn't let go.

Karly stood staring defiantly at us with her hands on her hips. Her boobs were about to pop out of her low-cut top. "Why don't you and your brain-dead boyfriend leave me alone?"

Alien Paul raised his arm and pointed at Karly. "You pushed this body over the cliff."

I stopped dead in my tracks. "What!" My hands clenched into fists. What did Alien Paul mean?

Nausea churned in my stomach. "Paul, what are you saying?"

Karly's eyes widened. "Stay away from me." She backed up, glaring at us.

I started to hyperventilate. I hated confrontation, but I wanted to slap her.

Karly pointed at me and smirked. "If you hadn't come into the picture, none of this would have happened."

"Why did you push Paul off the cliff?"

Tears came to her eyes as she crossed her arms and rocked on her heels. "I didn't mean to." She glared at Paul. "You made me so mad. You said that you loved me, and were going to end it with Skye. Then, you took her to Hunter's Point, our special place."

I turned to Paul. "Is this true?"

He nodded.

I turned back to Karly. "It was you. You were the stranger in the hoodie that day."

Karly's misty eyes shifted to Alien Paul. "When I saw you two together, I knew it would never end."

"But why did you push him?"

Karly's crocodile tears stained the makeup on her cheek. "It was an accident. I confronted Paul behind the bushes. We argued, and he twisted my wrist, bringing me to my knees. I was done with his verbal abuse and the beatings. I stood up and shoved him away. He ran after me and grabbed my arm so hard it felt like he pulled it out of the socket. I tried to fight him off, and we tumbled over the cliff. I grabbed hold of a branch and scrambled back up. You were calling for him. I got scared and ran home, thinking he was dead."

"You told me your dad beat you," I said.

"He made me," she said, pointing at Paul. "When you showed up, knocking at my door, he was hiding in the bedroom. He told me to say that my dad hit me, or I'd be sorry."

"Why didn't your dad protect you from Paul?" I asked.

"My dad only cares about his beer and cigarettes."

I staggered back and took a deep breath. How sick and twisted. I'd had a feeling from the beginning that there was something wrong with Paul. The abuse I took from him when we were kids. I chose to believe he had changed and trusted him. I should have acted on my intuitions but chose to be blind.

All lies—Paul intentionally lied to me about being with Karly and led me to believe that he was innocent of her accusations. He told me she was stalking him. I was a fool for believing him. A breeze blew a wisp of hair across my face, and I blinked.

Karly stepped toward Paul and touched his cheek. "I'm sorry you're messed up. It was an accident. We both got hurt." She turned and backed away, clutching her chest as she ran across the pier.

The only pain I felt was disappointment. The irony was that I'd doubted Alien Paul's sincerity. When all along, the real monster was the original Paul.

"Skye, I sense you are upset," Paul said.

"I trusted you . . . him."

His blue eyes burned. "I am sorry you are hurting."

He drew me tight against him, and I buried my head against his warm, solid chest. In his arms, I felt safe and protected. I lifted my head and wrapped my arms around his neck. His eyes were deep cobalt, making a tingle run down my spine. Then, tired of fighting my feelings, my lips found his and lingered, deep and wanting.

Before I could finish my thought, his hands cupped the sides of my face. His incredible blue eyes locked on mine, and he stared into my soul. Somewhere in the back of my mind, I kept repeating, he's not human . . . he's not human.

"I enjoy this method of mating," he said. His hand ran down my backside.

I pushed away. "You're moving too fast. I don't think you understand . . ."

"Did I do something wrong?"

I tried to control the smile on my face. "As a matter of fact, you've done everything right. But you have to understand all this stuff is new to me."

The blank expression on his face told me he didn't understand what I was saying.

Waves slapped at the dock, the wind whispered across the sea, and I thought about how to explain it to him. He studied my face, and I sighed. "I've never had sex. It sounds old-fashioned, I know."

He flashed a smile that told me what I said hadn't quite registered.

I smiled back. It was a subject for another day. He still had a lot to learn about human nature. We walked back, hand in hand, to find the van.

When I dropped Alien Paul at his house, he gave me one last lingering kiss before he went inside. When I pulled into the driveway at home, all the lights were on. Nana was waiting up for me.

She was in the kitchen baking bread. She looked up when she heard the click of my sandals on the wooden floor. I draped her wrap over the back of a kitchen chair. "Thanks for letting me borrow this. It worked out great."

"Did you two have a nice time, dear?" she asked as she kneaded dough on the kitchen island counter. Her hands were white with flour.

"Dinner was wonderful. We had surf and turf." I didn't bring up the waitress or Karly.

"Would you like a cup of hot chocolate or tea? This bread is almost ready for the oven." She brushed a strand of hair behind her ear, leaving a streak of white in its place.

A laugh escaped my lips. "Oh, Nana, you've got flour in your hair."

"Do I, dear?" Nana lifted her flour-covered hands off the counter, swiped them across both sides of her temples, and lifted her hair high. Then, she pivoted from side to side, batting her eyes. "Do I look like the Bride of Frankenstein?"

I ran over and gave her a big hug, and she patted my face, covering it with flour. We laughed and twirled. I loved her so much.

CHAPTER 16

THE MEANING OF LIFE

I went to bed that night with mixed emotions. Although I had feelings for Alien Paul, I wondered if his only agenda was to find a mate. Even though I found him the most interesting man I'd ever met, he had no idea how human relationships worked. However, I no longer felt guilty about cheating on the old Paul now that I knew he had abused Karly. I tossed and turned, exhausted from the emotional stress of the evening, until I finally drifted off to sleep.

The next morning, I threw on a knit top and jeans after a quick shower. The fall weather was too cool for shorts. I checked myself in the mirror and ran downstairs. In the kitchen, June Takamura, Nana's friend and neighbor, sat at the table. They shared steaming mugs of coffee and sweet rolls. When Paul and I were kids, he would ride his bike by her house, yelling, "June, June, show me your moon." At the time, I thought it was funny. Now—I knew it was sick.

June glanced up at me. Short and petite, she wore a black t-shirt with a gold peace sign, jeans, and tennis shoes. Her hair, streaked with gray, was in a ponytail.

June smiled. "You are looking good, Skye. Your Nana has been catching me up with what you've been up to lately."

"Up to?" I glanced at Nana and frowned.

Nana smiled back at me. "I mentioned how you have been helping Paul with his recovery. How well he has been doing because of you."

June steepled her fingers together. "Good karma rewards you when you help others."

I nodded, wondering if karma pertained to aliens. Like Nana, and many older folks on the coast, June was an aging hippie. They'd probably planned their beach retirement while sitting around smoking pot at Woodstock.

"Skye, grab a cup of coffee. Come sit and have a Danish. They're fresh and delicious. June picked them up at the Seaside Bakery down on the point."

I wanted to walk on the beach, but I took a mug from the cupboard and filled it from the pot. Then I scooted a chair out from under the table and sat. The two women stared at me with apprehension, making me wonder what was on their minds. I reached over for a sweet roll and absently bit into it.

Two loaves of fresh bread that Nana baked sat on the pine sideboard. A white wainscot backsplash held a wooden rack of knives that reflected the sunshine in the bright kitchen. Nana's kitchen was clean and orderly. A stack of farmhouse crates in the corner by the window held the overflow from the cabinets.

"I think we should take a trip to Phoenix and get your stuff," Nana said. "June and I discussed it, and she agreed to watch the house and water the plants while we're gone." Nana's hair still had traces of flour from last night.

"OK," I said.

Nana must have sensed the hesitation in my voice. "Is something wrong, dear? You don't want to go?"

"It's just going to be strange to go back home, rummaging through Mom's things and dredging up my old life. Am I being ridiculous?"

Nana shook her head. "No, honey. Of course not. We could always hire an estate sale company to clear out the house, but I think doing it yourself will help bring closure."

June stood. "I'll let you two talk this out. You don't need a third wheel. I'm here if you need anything. Take care of yourself, Skye."

"You too," I mumbled.

Nana walked June to the door, where they made small talk for a few minutes. When she returned, she sat back down, reached across the table, and took my hand. "You don't have to do this. We can hire someone to pack up everything and sell the house. I just thought you would like to get your things."

I leaned back, tucking my hair behind my ears. "No, Nana. You're right. I can't just let the house sit and rot. I've got to face my fear of going back."

"Good, then let's plan to go next week. We can ask Paul if he wants to go with us. He's strong, and we could use his help with the packing and lifting."

I got up, went over to Nana, leaned down, and kissed her cheek. "I'm going to run over to Paul's house and see if he'll come with us." I smiled, wondering what Alien Paul would think of Arizona.

The brilliant sun was bringing the temperature up, so I decided to walk. I slid on my black and white Chuck Taylors and headed out the door. The summer tourists had packed up and left, so I had the beach to myself.

I wondered if Phoenix would feel strange after all this time. I hadn't spoken to any of my old friends since before I'd left. Most had drifted away after Dad died. It's funny how death can drive a wedge between friends. Maybe it makes them aware that they could be next in line to lose a loved one. I shuddered, thinking about the looks of sympathy I got after the funeral. At school, a crowded room would become silent, replaced by whispers and sideways glances when I walked in. The way I was treated still burned in my mind. All that I wanted, all I needed, was to be treated like before.

After the service, Mom changed too. The life in her eyes faded into depression. Feeling sorry for herself, she refused to talk about Dad and ignored me. God, if she had quit taking those damn pills, she'd be alive today.

When I reached Alien Paul's house, the empty driveway told me Carolyn was at work. I went up to the porch and rang the bell. No answer. I checked the handle. It was unlocked, so I let myself in and went down the hall to Paul's room. The door was open. He sat engrossed in the MacBook on his desk. This alien had all the information of the world at his fingertips.

I went up behind him and tapped him on the shoulder. "Hi, Paul. I came over to ask if you would like to take a trip to Phoenix with Nana and me?"

He swiveled the chair around and flashed me his perfect smile. "I will accompany you. You are important to me. I will not let you go alone."

"We'll have a good time," I said, and a smile played at the corners of my mouth. "Are you finding lots of stuff on the internet?"

"This world has diversity and countless differences. Much love but also much hate. Abundant wealth and considerable poverty."

"What was it like that where you came from?" I went over and sat on the bed.

"Our civilization is a collective. We serve only ourselves. There are no leaders, no wealth, no poverty."

I leaned forward, fascinated. "Were you like us? I mean, did you resemble us, or were you different?" I wanted to know if he had a head with big black almond-shaped eyes like the alien shows on TV.

He raised an eyebrow, and the faint trace of a smile lit up his face. "We have two arms and two legs. Our brains are more advanced with a larger capacity than humans have. In most other aspects, we resemble you."

I brushed my fingers through my hair, relieved that he wasn't totally freaky in his old life. There was so much more I wanted to ask. "You came from a star outside our solar system. How come we resemble each other?"

"Nature is cyclical, with evolution occurring recurrently across the universe, although not necessarily simultaneously. Descendants of evolved organisms resemble their ancestors."

I scratched my head. "Are you saying that we are all basically the same?"

"Life is constant throughout the universe. However, some of us are more advanced in the evolutionary stage than others."

"How is that possible?"

"Did you know how the universe came to be?"

"The universe started as nothing, then it grew and exploded and shot out all the matter that exists now. The Big Bang Theory is what we learned in science class."

"All matter was created simultaneously, in the same place," Paul said. "The universe is constantly expanding. Stars and galaxies are born and die. Life is death, and death is life. Matter is energy which is neither created nor destroyed; it only changes from one form to another."

I scratched my head again trying to understand everything he was telling me.

"The universe is seeded by microbes that drift through space. This is called panspermia. Earth's oceans were filled with water from comets and asteroids that hit the Earth. These also carried cosmic microbes responsible for the development of life on Earth, my world, and on and on. Like sperm seeds an egg, microbes seed the planets if they can support life. Humans believe they are unique, but we are all carbon copies of each other."

There were so many questions I wanted to ask him. But the one I really wanted to ask—the one I wanted to know—was the one most important to me.

I leaned forward, cautioning him with my eyes. "Do you know what happens to us after we die?"

He leaned back in his chair and studied me with those beautiful blue eyes. Finally, he spoke. "Everything in the universe is connected to consciousness. The awareness that exists in all beings comes from the universe and returns after death, where it can stay or go back into another being. My consciousness or soul inhabits this body."

I shook my head. "Then there is no God?"

"It is a matter of interpretation. Is God the universe, or is the universe God? The idea of a Universal God is perceived as eternal, spiritual, and everlasting. The idea of a supreme being has been around forever."

"But what about heaven?"

"Heaven is the consciousness in the universe, where the souls that desire to stay exist. Our race decided to inhabit other bodies to avoid death."

"Does your race have any proof of heaven?" I asked.

"Only that the belief in an immortal soul and afterlife is standard in almost all cultures and civilizations throughout the universe."

"But that's not scientific proof," I said. "I want to know that my mom and dad's souls went to heaven. That their existence meant something, not just ashes scattered in the wind."

His smile made his eyes sparkle. "You took my entity and put it in this body. Is that not enough proof that a soul exists?"

"I never thought about it like that." I gazed into Paul's deep blue eyes and wondered if they were the windows to his soul.

As I left Paul's house and headed home, one thing was clear: my head was spinning. That evening, I called Carolyn to ask permission for Paul to accompany us to Phoenix. She thought it was a great idea. All that was left was to pick a date and pack.

I tossed and turned that night, burning with strange, twisted dreams. The worst involved my dad. In it, I heard the waves crashing on the shore. I tried to follow the sound, but something tugged on my hand, pulling me the other way. I didn't want to go back. Instead, I went toward the light shining from the shoreline.

"Skye, run!" Dad yelled. He kept tugging my arm, but I jerked hard and broke away, desperate to get to the light.

I ran down the beach, away from him. When I was far enough away, I turned. "Why, Dad?" I wanted to go to the light, but he kept trying to stop me.

Suddenly, a flash of light hit Dad, and he yelped, fell into the sand, and twitched on the ground.

"Dad!" I screamed.

Paul rose out of the ocean and summoned me to come to him. His eyes were dark, almond shaped. I took a step forward, and he sneered. He bared sharp pointed teeth.

"Leave your dad." His mouth formed an evil grimace and turned shark-like.

I couldn't fight his influence on me. It was too much—one step forward, the next, then another.

"Trust me." He beckoned me on.

Forgetting about my dad, I lunged forward and ran into his arms.

Paul's mouth unhinged like a trap, and his fangs sunk deep into my neck, striking my jugular vein. Blood erupted everywhere, and all I saw was death.

I screamed and bolted upright in bed.

The clock on the dresser flashed at 4:10 in the morning. I groaned, fell back on the bed, and pulled a pillow over my face.

•• 🐚 ••

CHAPTER 17

ROAD TRIP

We decided to leave for Phoenix the following Monday and planned to spend a week getting the house ready to sell. After Dad died, Mom and I donated his clothes to charity. It was going to be hard going through her things this time around.

As dawn broke over the beach, we loaded the van. Nana packed the red ice chest with water bottles and snacks. Alien Paul hefted the cooler into the back and jumped in beside it. Nana drove, and I rode shotgun. A few people waved as we drove through town. It wasn't hard to recognize Nana's lime green VW bus with peace signs on the bumper and a rainbow sticker on the rear window.

I must have dozed off, but my eyes flew open when the van came to a screeching halt. Was there an accident? I glanced around, getting my bearings. Nana's seat was empty. We were at a gas station off the highway. I turned and glanced in the back. Alien Paul sat erect on the bench seat, like a cardboard cutout.

"What happened? Where's Nana?"

"She had to use the bathroom," he replied.

"I might as well go while we're here," I unfastened my seat belt and opened the door. "Do you need to go?" I asked him.

"No. I will wait."

I walked across the parking lot and reached out to open the bathroom door. It flew open, almost hitting me.

Nana came rushing out. "Damn near peed my pants," she said. "I didn't think I would make the last few miles, almost pulled off on the side of the road. I should keep a porta-potty in the van."

I laughed. "My turn. Paul stayed in the van."

Minutes later, we got back in the van and onto the highway. I turned around to look at Paul. He stared back at me with his deep blue eyes. Was he reading my mind?

Nana turned her head to the back. "Paul, could you hand me a water bottle out of the ice chest?"

He unfastened his seat belt and leaned over the backseat. "Do you want one, Skye?" he asked.

"I'll wait. There's not much around here, and I might need to go again soon."

We reached Sacramento and stopped for lunch. Nana wanted breakfast and a cup of coffee, so we pulled into a Denny's. The first thing we did was head for the bathroom. A waitress seated us in a booth and took our order. She had a hard time keeping her eyes off Paul.

Since Paul always ordered what I did, we settled on Grand Slams, scrambled, and coffee. The server brought our drinks, and Paul emptied three packets of cream and two sugars in his coffee.

Nana leaned across the table. "Did you notice how the waitress has taken to Paul?"

I shook my head. "It seems like a common occurrence lately. It must be his blue eyes. He never had that problem when they were brown."

Nana chuckled. "Those eyes make you quite the Casanova."

He knitted his brows together. "What does that mean?"

"It means you're a hunk." Nana winked at him, then turned to me. "I keep forgetting about his brain injury."

After lunch, we piled back in the van and headed for Bakersfield. We had another three hundred miles to cover on Interstate 5. I offered to drive, and Nana didn't argue. Since she wanted to take a nap, Paul rode up front. After a while, I heard her snoring in the back.

Paul watched me drive. It wasn't easy to concentrate on the road while feeling his gaze on my face.

He leaned toward me, the trace of a smile playing across his lips. "Teach me to drive."

I took my eyes off the road to see if he was serious. "When we get home, I'll help you practice driving. Paul had his license, so you don't need a permit. You will have to be careful not to get in an accident."

He leaned back and crossed his arms. "My reflexes are much more advanced than humans. My strength and endurance will be advantageous in mastering the automobile."

My eyes speared him. "You need to be careful. If you crash the car, you can be hurt or killed. Extra strength doesn't mean you're invincible."

He rippled his shoulders and laughed. "I am not afraid."

My fingers white-knuckled the steering wheel. It upset me that Paul could be insensitive to my feelings about death, and risk his life. He was acting like a macho jerk. I glanced over at him. He was staring out the window, back to being the docile alien. I sighed. After all, he saved me from the riptide. My anger faded into gratitude.

Nana woke from her nap, needing to use the bathroom again. A rest stop was coming up, so I veered off the ramp. We all got out, and I locked the van. It felt good to stretch my legs.

When I came out of the bathroom, I spotted Paul by a tourist billboard. I walked over and noticed he was fiddling with a soft drink machine. He raised his head and gave me a faint smile.

I smiled back. "Hey, what are you doing?"

His fingers danced across the money slot, and a soda can rolled out the bottom. "I wanted a drink." He pulled the can from the bin, popped the tab, and put it to his lips.

"Did you pay for that?" I asked.

He fluttered his fingers in front of my face. "No need. I manipulated the circuit board."

I crossed my arms and glared at him. "That's stealing."

He raised an eyebrow. "Stealing?"

"Yes. Taking something that doesn't belong to you. They put people in jail for stealing."

He held up the can and laughed. "This is insignificant. They would not punish me for taking this drink."

I frowned. "Maybe not. But first, it's a soda from a machine. Next, it's money from an ATM. You can't be doing this. Just ask if you want a soda, and I'll give you money to pay for it."

He glanced over his shoulder. Nana was walking toward us.

"We'll talk about this later," I whispered. Nana didn't need to know about his strange talent.

Nana sat on the bench by the machine. "I've been looking all over for you. I went back to the van, but you had the keys. Are you ready to go?"

"Sorry, Nana. Paul wanted a drink." I gave him a sideways glance.

Back at the van, I handed Nana the keys so she could drive the rest of the way to Bakersfield. I rode shotgun, and Paul climbed in the back.

Nana reserved two adjoining rooms at the Quality Inn in Bakersfield. After we checked in, we put our stuff in our rooms. Nana and I had a room with two queen beds. Paul's room, right next door, had a king bed. I was so tired from the long drive that I didn't care if I slept in a sleeping bag on the floor.

The following morning, we packed the van, gassed up, and headed toward Barstow.

The scenery turned to desert, much like Phoenix. Then, after about a hundred miles, the sign for Interstate 15 finally appeared. I pulled out my phone and searched for points of interest around Barstow.

"This is interesting." I read: "The Calico Early Man site, located outside the town of Barstow, where prehistoric tools were found embedded in the shoreline of an ancient lakebed called Lake Manix."

Paul reached over my seat from the back and grabbed the phone out of my hand. "Hey, I'm not done reading," I yelled.

He sat back, and his fingers danced across the screen. His eyes glowed cobalt as he read the text. "This article claims that humans settled on the shores of the ancient lake more than 30,000 years ago," Paul said.

He reached out and shoved the phone back at me. "We have to go there."

Nana pulled off on the shoulder and turned off the motor. She unbuckled her belt and turned to Paul. "We don't have time to stop and sightsee. We need to get to Phoenix."

Wondering what had gotten into Paul, I unfastened my belt and looked at him as well. "Nana's right. We could lose another day if we stop there."

He leaned forward and clenched his hands into fists. Then, his eyes flared. "I need to see the archeological site. It is important to me."

Nana's lined face settled into a scowl. "Enough of this nonsense, Paul. We have a long way to travel."

"Then leave me there and go on your way." Paul leaned back in the seat and crossed his arms.

"You're acting like a defiant child," Nana said. Her blazing eyes told me she wouldn't be easily swayed.

"Leave me there," he fumed from the backseat.

I leaned forward, cautioning him with my eyes, not wanting him to push Nana too far. "What's so important about that place?"

"Intuition. I cannot say until I walk the prehistoric lakebed."

Nana looked at me and shook her head. "I can't figure him out. I hope he's not having a relapse from his brain injury."

Knowing how determined Alien Paul was and how stubborn Nana could be, I decided to end this stand-off. I brushed my hair behind my ears and let out a sigh.

"What's one more day if it means so much to Paul? He doesn't ask for much."

Nana exhaled. "If I could only wrap my mind around why it's so important, I wouldn't have a problem going. She scowled at Paul. "And I won't be bullied." Then, Nana turned around in her seat, straightened her collar, and started the engine. "Next stop, the Calico Early Man site."

"Thanks, Nana." I glanced back at Paul. He had a determined look on his face.

We pulled back onto the interstate, and I went to the internet to get directions for Nana. It was close to noon, so we decided to pick up lunch at a drive-through and take it with us.

When we arrived, a dirt road led to the site. The old VW van bumped along. Finally, we crested a hill and drove up to a "CLOSED" sign on a locked gate. Paul slid the rear door open and jumped out.

Nana yelled out the window, "Paul, where are you going? It's closed." She looked over at me and rolled her eyes. "What's gotten into that boy?"

Paul was too busy fiddling with the lock to answer Nana. It popped free, and he slid the gate open. "Come on," he shouted.

"That's breaking and entering," Nana called back. "I want no part of this. Get back in the van."

Paul ran to the van and lifted the tailgate. He rummaged through the back and pulled out his gray day pack and a tire iron. He slammed the rear hatch shut, ran off through the gate, and disappeared up a hill.

Nana blew out a breath. "I'm too old to be chasing after that crazy boy."

I opened my door. "I'll go after him. You wait here, and I'll be back as soon as possible. I've got my cell. I'll call you if anything happens or I can't find him."

Nana looked worried. "Take some water from the chest, Skye. And be careful."

I went into the back, got out my day pack, and loaded it with several water bottles. "See you in a while. Don't worry, I'll find him."

I trudged off up the hill in Paul's direction. When I reached the top, I had a view of the entire valley below. Paul was down in a depression, off in the distance; that must have been Lake Manix.

I took off in a sprint down a dusty path. I had to stop at the bottom of the hill and catch my breath. He was still in the same spot out on the dry lakebed. I pulled a water bottle from the pack, chugged it down, and started off in Paul's direction.

When I caught up to him, he had dug a hole about five feet deep with the tire iron in the hard-packed soil. He was lying on his stomach, reaching into the hole.

A gust of wind whipped my hair back off my face. "Paul, what are you doing?"

"Skye, hold my feet so I can reach further in." His voice echoed from the pit.

I got down on my knees and held his ankles. He shimmied further into the hole. I crawled along until his weight became almost unbearable.

A dark object covered in dirt flew out of the hole and landed in the sand.

"Skye, pull me up," he hollered.

I pulled back as hard as possible, and he crawled out of the hole. Dirt matted his face and arms. Finally, he stood up, went over to the object on the ground, and held it up for me to see.

"Do you recognize this?" He held it closer.

I blinked, brushed my hair aside, and studied the object. It was dark and crusted with dirt. The shape was familiar, oval-shaped with a row of spines. A musky rancid smell drifted from it, suffocating me. I swallowed and rubbed my damp palms on my shorts. Yes, I remembered it. The dark silhouette was like the seashell I found on the beach. Only this one was sinister. And smelly. My heart thumped in my chest.

I studied Paul. "A seashell. Like your shell, but it's evil. I can feel it." I rubbed my arms, shivering.

Paul stared at the shell in his hand. "Yes, evil."

I gazed at the hideous object and wet my lips. "What does it mean?"

He looked at me, and his eyes flashed sapphire. "The Bahlari have been here."

CHAPTER 18

CHASING THE DEVIL

As I stared at the dark shell, I fought the urge to rip it from Paul's hand so I could throw it back in the pit. I sensed that inside the evil shell was a place where monsters might lurk. Icy fear crept through my body, and I shivered in the heat of the desert sun. My heart raced against my chest, and I backed away. I was afraid then, afraid to ask about the Bahlari.

Paul's finger traced the shell's ridges. "This archeological site confirms what I suspected. The Bahlari traveled to various destinations on this planet. They were not contained to one area." His voice was sober.

"How did you know where to find the shell?"

"This was an early human settlement site. The Bahlari seek out humans to create chaos and destruction. They, in turn, feed off the fear they generate. This shell is one of the portals they used to access this world."

"Why do you want to keep it?"

"It was the device they traveled through to arrive here. It is also a means to track their location."

"Why do you want to find them? Aren't they dangerous?"

"Extremely dangerous. They are aware of my presence now that I am liberated from the shell. I am newly arrived. This is my first host body. They will perceive me as a threat."

"Why would they single you out? You said there are others of your kind here."

"The others have been on this planet for nearly a hundred years. They would have had to transfer host bodies more than once in that time."

"I still don't understand why you would be a threat to them."

"Each host body that accepts our entity affects us. Over time, we become more like the species we inhabit. The others have become more human than our original entity. It is a danger the scouts must endure if they remain long enough on a planet."

"So, you're saying that each body you inhabit dilutes your species?"

"Yes. The longer we remain, the more hosts we inhabit. Eventually, we lose the memory of our entity and become fully absorbed into the race we populate. The others that traveled with me may have no recollection of their origins, depending on how many times they transferred bodies. Some might have inherited several before finally arriving in a stable life form."

"Stable life form?"

"One that lives a long life and does not perish early from a fatal mishap or disease."

I glanced down at the shell in his hand. "Do you still feel Paul inside?" I asked. "After what you just said, he has to be a part of you."

"He looms in the background of my mind. His presence is faint."

"Oh," I sighed, uncertain what to think. Unsure of everything.

He brushed his hand across my cheek. "I could not restore Paul, but my presence saved his life. You must not feel regret for placing my entity inside."

"I don't regret putting you in him. There was nothing else I could do. I've grown to care deeply for you." My eyes blurred. Was I confusing kindness with love?

Paul moved closer until my cheek was against his chest. I clung to him and let the tears flow. He gently stroked my hair as I wept.

"We better get back," Paul said. "Hand me my pack."

I reached down, shook off the desert sand, and gave it to him.

I slipped it off my shoulders and gave it to him. He tugged the zipper and dropped the shell inside. He put the straps through his arms, and we started making our way back to the path to the road. While we staggered up the hill, I fought off waves of nausea, thinking about the evil aliens and what they could do to Alien Paul.

We stopped at the crest of the hill, and I stared back at the long flat plain below. Paul's breath unraveled into a sigh, and I got a faint whiff of his powder scent. Far down in the desert, surrounded by brown mountains, waterless Lake Manix shimmered in the hot desert sun.

When we reached the open gate, I saw Nana lying in the van with the rear door open, reading a book. Paul slid the gate shut and refastened the lock. Nana put her book down and headed our way. The look on her face told me to intervene before she reached Paul. I surged forward. "Nana, wait!" I sputtered.

She strong-armed me aside. "Paul and I are going to have a little Come-to-Jesus talk. So, honey, you go and sit in the van."

There was no way I was going to sit in the van. I stood rooted to the ground. I had to hear what was being said.

Alien Paul was sliding the pack off his shoulders. He glanced up and saw Nana approaching. He must have sensed her mood because he dropped the bag to the ground.

Nana stood between Paul and the pack; her hands clenched into fists. "Listen, Mister. You have a lot of explaining to do. What's the idea of taking off like that?"

Paul looked down at the pack, ignoring Nana's ranting. This only made her more furious. "Well, answer me!"

He glanced up. "There was something I needed to see."

Nana pushed her hair back from her face and stomped her foot. "Something you needed to see. You put Skye in danger. She went looking for you. What if she got lost? You had no right to run off . . ." Nana stopped ranting midsentence, and her eyes riveted on the pack at Paul's feet. She reached down for the strap, then froze. She swallowed, then snatched up the bag.

"No, Nana." Dread flooded through my veins as I rushed forward to stop her.

Paul reached out and pinched the tab on top of the pack, pulling it toward him, but Nana wouldn't let go. I clutched the other strap in my hand. "Nana, let go!"

The seam on the pack ripped, and the crusted black shell fell at our feet. A rancid musky smell drifted up from the ground. Nana let go of her end of the pack and gagged. She turned to me with her hand over her mouth, and tears flooded her eyes.

Paul reached down, plucked the offensive shell from the ground, and wrapped it in the torn pack. He clutched the wad tight in his fists.

"What the hell is that?" Nana gasped. She looked at Paul, then at me, and back again. Apparently, Paul wasn't going to answer. I looked at him and shrugged my shoulders. "It's what Paul was looking for, out in the dry lakebed."

"What is it?" Nana fixed Paul with a glare. "It stinks, and it creeps me out."

Paul silently returned her stare. I guessed it was up to me. I frowned and shook my head. It seemed that this alien with superpowers who had saved my life was intimidated by Nana.

"Nana! Paul and I need to talk to you right away."

"OK, but let's talk in the van," Nana said. "We've wasted too much time here. We won't get to Flagstaff until after dark."

Paul and I followed Nana to the van. She opened the driver's side door and turned to him. "Leave that smelly thing here. I don't want it in the van with us."

Paul clutched the bag tighter. "It must accompany us. I need it."

Nana walked over and grabbed at the wadded-up pack. "It stays here."

"No, Nana. He's in danger. Listen to what we have to say."

Nana crossed her arms and let out a sigh. "Talk to me."

I stepped forward. "Remember when I told you about the shell?"

Nana nodded her head. "The shell you took to the hospital? When Paul woke up from the coma?"

"Yes. I told you the truth. The alien inside the shell got inside Paul's head."

Paul stepped closer. "Skye speaks the truth. My entity was the reason he woke up from the coma. I traveled from light-years away. We departed through a vortex in a helix that transported us to this world."

Nana frowned. "How did you survive? Traveling all that way to arrive here."

"We shed our bodies and converted to molecules that allowed us to survive the passage. You call it a soul. Our entities were in stasis until we arrived inside shells in the ocean."

Nana shook her head and laughed. "I never thought aliens would show up in a seashell. I always imagined a starship would herald their arrival."

Paul glared at Nana. "This is not fantasy. I am in danger."

I studied Nana's face, struggling to read what she was thinking about all this.

"How are you in danger?"

"The Bahlari, the aliens that came to this planet long ago. They traveled through the dark shells. They are malevolent . . . evil, intent on destroying humanity."

Nana's face softened. "Your brain injury could be causing these delusions, Paul. Just because your brown eyes turned blue isn't a reason to assume you're an alien."

"My entity is inside this body."

"Then prove it!" Nana demanded.

Alien Paul unwrapped the pack and took out the hideous shell. He threw the bag aside, put the shell between his palms, and rubbed it back and forth like sticks to start a fire.

We remained silent, watching his strange show.

A dark funnel cloud grew out of the shell, producing a cyclone that hovered above our heads. In the center of the black cloud, hundreds of stars appeared.

Nana staggered back against the van. The wind created by the flume blew faster and faster, whipping our hair across our faces.

"Paul, stop," I screamed.

He stopped rotating the shell and held his hands up toward the sky. Finally, the cyclone retreated inside the shell, and all was calm.

"Oh, my God." Nana pushed away from the van and stumbled into my arms.

Paul picked up the pack and wrapped the shell back inside. "There is not much time."

Nana lifted her head from my shoulder and looked at Paul. "Not much time for what?"

"I must find the other portals. The Bahlari are in a position to destroy the Earth, and I must find a way to stop them. Leave me here and go on to Phoenix."

A cold air pocket made me shiver. "Don't leave me."

"When my mission is complete, I will meet you back in California," he promised.

I broke from Nana and ran to him. "I'm going with you."

He touched my arm and brought his face close to mine. His eyes were serious. "I will not put you in danger or be responsible for your death. I must go alone."

"You are the cause, the reason I'm here—alive."

"What are you talking about?" Nana stumbled forward, a worried look in her eyes.

I turned to her. "He rescued me from drowning in the riptide."

"You never mentioned . . ." she put her hands on her hips. "When? And why didn't you tell me?"

"Ever since this Alien Paul thing happened, there's a lot I've kept hidden. Now that it's out in the open, I don't have to lie anymore."

Nana smoothed her wind-blown hair and nodded, telling me she understood. How could she not, after what she'd just witnessed?

I turned to Paul, wrapped my arms around his waist, and laid my head on his shoulder. "What will you do? You don't have a vehicle or any money."

The muscles in his shoulders rippled. "I have survived this long without possessions."

I pulled away. "But you've had people help you since you've been in Paul's body. Me, Carolyn, Jeff, and Nana. You were never left alone to fend for yourself. I want to go with you." I gazed into his eyes, pleading.

I watched his chest rise and fall. He wasn't going to answer; that much was clear.

"Do you want me to go away?"

He held my gaze, then looked away. "It will be dangerous. I do not know if I can keep you safe." His eyes flashed sapphire blue.

Right then, I knew he would take me with him.

I turned to Nana. "I'm going with Paul. We can drop you off at the nearest airport if you let us take the van."

Nana planted her hands on her generous hips, and her nostrils flared. "Like hell, you will."

"Please, Nana," I said. "We need the van to get around. I'm too young to rent a car."

"You're not taking me anywhere. I'm going with you." A smile escaped Nana's lips. "I wouldn't miss this for the world."

"But you heard Paul; he said it's dangerous." I tried to hide my smile.

"If you're willing to stick your neck out, so am I. Paul may have superhuman powers, but those aliens have a fight on their hands with your old Nana," she said with determination.

I turned to Paul and shrugged. "I guess we stick together."

He squared his chiseled chin. "We need to go somewhere and devise a plan," he said, with a haunted look in his eyes.

WHO GOES THERE?

Nana checked us in at the Travel Lodge in Barstow and booked two adjoining rooms. We stopped on the way and picked up Subway. Inside the room, we spread our feast across the table and sat down to dig in.

After we ate, I turned on all the lights to drive out the impending darkness. Then, catching my reflection in the dark motel window, I closed the heavy drapes. Dusk silhouetted the rocky desert mountains across the silent parking lot, making them look like strange, king-sized sandcastles. I crossed my arms over my chest and shivered.

"Come and sit, Skye," Nana called. "We need to know what we're up against."

I let go of the fabric, the curtain fell back in place, and I turned to join them at the table.

Paul leaned forward and put his hands on the table. "In ancient times, humans roamed the plains as hunter-gatherers in tribes, taking their food and shelter where they could find it. Animals and vegetation were plentiful. There was no need for fighting or war. Earth was a virtual Garden of Eden, as stated in the Bible."

Nana asked, "How do you know all this? The way things were . . . the Bible?"

Paul raised his deep blue eyes that glowed with an inner light. "Google Search. I have studied your religion and history on the internet, among many other subjects. Before we arrived, I and the others who accompanied me to Earth had acquired some knowledge of the human race."

"How long ago was that?" I asked.

"We arrived in the year 1933. Twelve of my people and I were assigned to track the Bahlari on this planet. Unfortunately, my shell became buried under the ocean before I could escape."

Nana rubbed her forehead. "What do the Bahlari want with us?"

"The Bahlari brought darkness and evil to this planet. Their entities traveled here through the vortex and could not bring weapons or machines. Once established on Earth, through human interaction, the Bahlari caused wars, toppled civilizations, and crushed religions. But they had no access to weapons of mass destruction."

"Why wait until 1933 to send scouts to track the Bahlari on Earth?" Nana asked.

"After the first World War, humans made strides in advancing sciences. However, over the last century, nuclear power, atomic bombs, and other advanced technology have set the stage for the Bahlari to gather weapons of mass destruction to end humanity. The tension brewing in Germany was escalating. The Nazis, powered by the Bahlari, were building dominance and control in Europe. So, the emissaries of our world sent us to evaluate the situation."

"Wouldn't the Bahlari also destroy themselves in the process?" Nana asked.

"They can transport their entities to other worlds and start the entire process all over again."

"It doesn't make sense," I said. "Why would the Bahlari destroy this world just to move to another?"

"Exactly," Nana agreed.

"The Bahlari's objectives are to create chaos and the absolute annihilation of civilizations throughout the universe."

"Can you contact your scouts that are still on Earth?" I asked.

Paul went to the fridge and took out a water bottle. "I do not sense their location." He twisted the bottle open and took a long swig. "Perhaps a safety measure, so the Bahlari cannot track them."

"Can't you read their minds through telepathy?" I asked.

He set the bottle on the counter. "I receive random jumbled signals, but I cannot determine the position of the transmission."

A chill blew through the room, even though all the windows were closed. The curtains fluttered, and I felt the strangest sensation that something was in the room with us.

A loud thump on the door made us jump. Paul motioned for Nana and me to go through the door into his room. I shook my head and stood my ground, not about to go anywhere if he was in trouble. If this was war, I'd signed up as a recruit. A soldier doesn't run at the first sign of danger. Nana must have felt the same; she stood rooted to the floor with her arms crossed over her chest.

Paul put his finger to his lips, went over to the window, and drew the curtain back. "No one is out there," he said.

He turned toward the door and unlatched the deadbolt. Nana and I stood behind him while he opened the door. We moved out onto the porch. A dead crow was lying on the stoop.

Paul shook his head and sucked in a breath. "The Bahlari have found me."

Nana stepped forward, "It's just a crow. The light from the window must have attracted it, and it flew into the door."

I reached back and pulled the door closed. "But the drapes were closed. It's pitch black out here." I pulled the door open, and light spilled out onto the dark entry, proving my point.

Paul stooped down to examine the bird, then stood and kicked the carcass into the shrubs. He turned and held an object up to the light. "This was clutched in its claw."

A shiver ran down my spine. It was a tiny black sea-shell—a miniature of the one Paul had found in the desert.

I swallowed. "What are we going to do?"

"Now, wait a minute." Nana stepped forward. "This could be a coincidence. There must be millions of those shells out in the desert. After all, it's a dried-up lakebed. Crows are curious creatures; they often carry off trash and debris."

"They are also associated with death and darkness. An emissary for the Bahlari to track me down."

A chill passed through me. "Let's go back inside," I said, rubbing my arms. Nana and Paul followed me into the room, and I locked the door.

"We must leave at first light," Paul said.

"Where are we going? Don't you have to search for the Bahlari?" I said.

"Not anymore. They have found me," Paul said.

"Then where will we go?" Nana said.

"They will seek me out wherever I go."

"Let's get some sleep, and we'll talk about it in the morning," Nana said.

Paul came over, put his arms around me, and looked at Nana. "I want to keep the door between our rooms open in case there is trouble tonight."

Nana and I nodded in agreement.

I had a hard time sleeping that night. I lay on my back, watching the ceiling, waiting for something to happen.

I drifted off and then came awake. Nana snored softly in her bed. I crawled out from under the covers and went to the open doorway to look in on Paul. He was at the window, listening, looking out with his head cocked. The dim light from the parking lot and shadows gave his face the appearance of an exhausted mask.

My heart skipped a beat; I knew he was worried. I entered the room and whispered his name so I wouldn't startle him. He turned from the window and raised an eyebrow. I inched closer, and he put his arms around me and brushed his face against my hair.

"This is bad," I whispered. "Worse than you thought."

He lifted my chin and studied my face. "I warned you of the danger. The Bahlari have no issue with you. They want me. You and your grandmother should go home."

I threw my arms around him and hugged him close. "Almost everyone I love is dead. If anything happens to you, I don't want to live." I reached up behind his neck, drew his lips to mine, and kissed him. Not tender but pleading . . . *please don't leave me.*

The rest of that night, I lay with Paul on his bed. Our bodies were pressed against each other—the rise and fall of his chest against my back. The familiar aroma of powder made me realize how much I now loved this man from another world. There was no way he was getting out of my sight.

The light of dawn crept through the heavy drapes. I lay cradled in his arms, dazed. I moaned and rolled over, knowing it was time to get up but wanting to stay against his side.

His arm pulled me back to bed, and I leaned back into him. He snuggled against me, his fingers tracing my stomach, sending a shiver through me.

The door between our rooms slammed shut. Paul leaped from the bed, almost knocking me to the floor. He ran to the door, pushed against it, and wrestled with the handle.

Nana's muffled screams rang out from the next room. "Get away . . . Get off me . . ."

Unable to open the door, Paul turned and unlocked the front door and tore outside. I was right behind him.

CHAPTER 20

AN EYE FOR AN EYE

The motel door stood wide open, and I could hear Nana's piercing screams. Paul charged through the door with me in tow. A flock of crows swarmed Nana. She thrashed on the bed, flailing her hands out to defend herself from the attacking birds.

Some of the crows swooped, striking me. I fell to the floor, throwing my arms up to protect my face. Their sharp claws cut swatches across my bare skin.

Through my fingers, I saw Paul run over to Nana, smacking the crows out of the way. She had kicked the covers off the bed in the struggle to fend off the birds. Paul ripped the comforter off the floor and covered her with it from head to toe.

He pulled me out of the room, motioning me to stay outside, then ran into his room. Where was he going?

As I watched from the doorway, Paul shot back into the room as the crows pecked at the comforter that covered Nana. The stuffing inside the quilt was all over the room.

"Paul, we have to do something," I shouted.

Paul raised his hands toward the ceiling with the black shell from the desert clutched in his fist. As he whirled it in the air, a cyclone escaped the shell and soared through the room. As it built momentum, the wind twirled the birds into a vortex, faster and faster, sucking them into the shell.

The cyclone's suction whipped the quilt off Nana's body, joining the vortex with the crows. Uncovered, Nana lay paralyzed, screaming on the bed. A crow hovered over her face, reached down, and pecked out her eyeball. I raced over, shrieking, and smacked it away, as hard as I could.

The bird fell to the floor, dead, with Nana's eyeball clutched in its beak.

I backed away and threw my hand over my mouth to keep from throwing up.

Paul ran over to Nana's bed, covered the bloody wound where her eye had been with his palm, and applied pressure. Nana moaned and writhed on the bed under his grip.

"Skye, get her eyeball," Paul yelled from Nana's bed.

My eyes moved to the crow on the floor with the hideous bloody eye in its beak, then back at Paul. I felt sick. My knees buckled; I was afraid I would pass out. "We need to call 911. Nana needs an ambulance."

"Skye, get her eye and give it to me," Paul repeated.

The urgency in his voice made me pull my eyes away from the horror on the floor. It was staring at me. Nana's eyeball, clutched in the crow's beak—was staring at me.

"Skye. Get her eye. I cannot release the pressure. She will bleed out," Paul said.

I tore my eyes from the floor and stumbled to grab a box of tissues on the nightstand.

I pulled them, one after the other, and kept pulling them out until the box was empty. Then, clutching the bundle in my fist, I staggered over to the hideous black form. Looking away, I blindly reached out with the wad of tissues. I pried the eyeball out of its beak, fighting back the urge to vomit.

I forced my way over to Paul with the bloody eye clenched in the tissue. I held it out and looked away.

He took the wadded mess from my hand. "Get me a wet towel," he said.

I pulled a face towel from the rack in the bathroom and ran it under warm water in the sink. I froze when I carried the wet towel out the door to give to Paul. He was hovering over Nana; her eyeball cupped in the palm of his hand. She lay motionless on the bed. Was she dead?

Paul smacked his palm hard against her eye socket, and I shrieked.

He ignored me and pushed hard against Nana's cheek. A red glow blazed from under his cupped hand, where it pressed against Nana's face.

Paul seemed to be in a trance. His head rolled from side to side in a circular motion. As he did, the light under his hand became brighter and brighter. It burned my eyes, and I turned away.

It was so brilliant I could see my shadow thrown against the wall. The dazzling light intensified and burst across the room like a flare from the sun. I threw my hands up over my eyes and screamed, afraid of being burned, but there was no heat.

The room dimmed, and I turned back to the bed. Nana was lying still with the wet towel over her eyes. Paul stood by her, shaking his hand back and forth like he was in pain.

I moved forward. "What just happened?"

"Nana was in shock. I had to put her to sleep," he said.

I went to the bed, picked up her still-cold hand, and put it in mine. "We have to get her to the hospital."

"When she wakes up, she will be fine," he said.

I set Nana's hand on the bed. "Fine? It tore her eye out. She's not going to be fine." I turned on my heel. "I'm calling 911."

Paul's hand whipped out and grasped my wrist. I tried to pull away, but his grip was firm.

"Let go of me."

"Skye, calm down." He spun me around, pulled me to the bed, and jerked the towel from Nana's face.

Nana looked healed. There was no blood, no scars. I whirled on Paul. "How did you do that?"

He raised his palm, a faint smile on his face. "Healing powers."

"Like the soda machine and the locks?"

He smiled wider and nodded with a twinkle in his eyes. He reminded me of a star quarterback who had just won a game.

I fell into him, put my arms around his waist, and squeezed tight. "Oh, Paul. Is she really going to be OK?"

A thought crossed my mind. "Can she see?"

He beamed. "Just like before."

"What about the trauma of what happened to her?" I whispered.

"I fixed that too. She won't remember that the crow attacked her, only the birds flying around the room."

I threw my arms around his waist and covered his face with kisses. "Thank you . . . thank you . . . thank you . . ." My lips found his and lingered.

Afterward, he put his face in my hair and whispered, "You make me feel human."

Pulling back, I smoothed my hair and gazed into the beauty of his kind blue eyes. "By coming into my life, you have also given me something. First, you pulled me out of the darkness of the death of my parents. Then you saved my life, and now you've saved Nana's. I am grateful for everything you have brought into my life."

We kissed again. My tears soaked the collar of his shirt, but he didn't seem to mind.

I pulled back. "We'd better get something to eat. We didn't have any breakfast. I'll run out while you stay with Nana."

"I am not letting you out of my sight after what happened this morning. We stay together," he said.

"Then I'll call for delivery. Should we wake Nana? She hasn't eaten."

"Let her sleep. She has been through a lot and needs to heal. We can save something for her to eat when she wakes up."

I searched through my phone. Domino's was the only place offering delivery in the area. So, I ordered two large pizzas. Who knows how long we'd be holed up in this room? Better to have too much than not enough.

An hour later, there was a rap at the door. I got up to answer it, but Paul held me back and went to the window. Satisfied, he opened the door and gave the driver the cash I handed him.

He carried the pizza boxes to the table, and I passed out napkins. We ate in silence. My stomach was still reeling from the morning's horror fest.

After what happened, we decided to stay in Nana's room. Paul bolted the door to his room, and we sat on my bed and turned on the TV. We propped ourselves up with pillows against the headboard, and I stared at the screen, not paying attention.

Paul's hand rested on my leg. I studied his long fingers and the muscles that ran along his arm and wondered what other powers he possessed. Groggy and full, I scooted down and laid my head against his chest as he stroked my hair.

I closed my eyes, and a dark memory struggled to break into my consciousness. The same one that had haunted me since Mom died. I tried to force the ghosts of the past away, but the terrible guilt and sadness refused to leave my heart.

My mind drifts back to Nana's cottage on the beach. I peer into the lamplit living room where Mom is lying on the couch. As I approach the sofa, Mom sits up. "Skye, I want to talk to you."

I sit in a green padded wicker chair across from her. "What's up?"

"Listen, Skye. You've been under a lot of stress. You need to relax and get some sleep. Let me give you one of my pills. It will calm you."

I stand and clench my fists in anger. "Which one, Mom? Elavil, Valium, Ativan, or Ambien?" I scream. "Don't look so shocked. I searched them on the internet. You're not supposed to take all those pills together. I'm surprised you haven't killed yourself yet."

She stares back at me with the most hurtful expression of hopelessness I have ever seen in her eyes. Mom throws herself on the couch and curls up in a fetal ball.

"I'm not trying to hurt you, Mom," I plead. "But I don't know what else to do. Ever since Dad died, I don't know how to please you or make you happy." I touch her shoulder. "Mom, you need help. You're not doing anything about your addiction."

Mom cringes away from my touch, pulling herself tighter into a ball against the back of the couch. "Go away, leave me alone," she moans like a spoiled child.

Her childlike response fuels my anger. "Do you want to turn me into a zombie? Like you?" I hope I haven't gone too far, but she needs a wake-up call.

"I was only trying to help," her muffled voice says to the back of the sofa.

"I don't want your pills. I want you to be here for me. Fat chance of that happening."

I storm out of the house and take a walk on the beach to calm my anger.

That night, I tiptoe upstairs to Mom's bedroom and crack the door. Inside the dark room, Mom is weeping in her bed. I stand at the door, wanting to comfort her but unwilling to apologize for what I said. Unsure of what to do for her, I gently close the door and tiptoe back to my room . . .

"Skye, wake up. Wake up." Paul was shaking me.

"What, what's wrong?" I moaned and rolled toward him, opening my eyes.

"You were dreaming," he said.

I struggled up from sleep, my skin clammy with sweat and my heart beating fast. Then the horror flooded back into my awareness, and I bolted upright in the bed. I wiped the sleep from my eyes. "It wasn't a dream. It was the last time I saw my mom alive. It haunts me, plays in my head, over and over again."

His fingers traced my cheek. "I sensed it while you slept."

We sat looking into each other's eyes, and I let out a breath. "Then you know that I was responsible for her death?"

He pulled me close. "It was not your fault. She was on a path to self-destruction. You told her yourself that you were surprised she was still alive."

"But that day . . . what I said . . . it pushed her over the edge. She took her own life. I never had time to apologize. The next morning, she was dead." Tears ran down my cheeks.

I turned and grabbed his shoulders. "Paul, I've got an idea. Do to me what you did to Nana. Make me forget that day."

Paul's finger reached out, trailed my wet cheek, and brushed it across his lip. "Sweet and salty. Contrasts."

I blinked. "What?"

Human emotions are contrasts and opposites. Right and wrong, sweet and sour, good and evil. Nothing is perfect."

"I don't understand?" I stammered.

"Your mother chose to jump off the cliff. You did not push her. You tried to open her eyes, but she refused to see. Her pain consumed her. There was no other option in her mind."

"But I still feel guilty about getting mad and yelling at her and not telling her I loved her before she died."

He stroked my hair. "She knows you loved her. She might have closed her eyes, but she was not blind."

I inched closer and leaned into his chest. "I wish I could believe that," I whispered.

"Everything that happens in our lives cultivates our character. If I erase the bad memories, then all that is left is good. There is nothing to be gained and no lesson learned with only the affirmative."

"But you did it for Nana."

"She experienced a traumatic event. Nana is a resilient human, but having her eye ripped out by the crow could have damaged her psyche for the rest of her life. I spared her that pain."

I smiled and hugged him tightly. "I'm glad I found such a wise alien in that seashell."

Paul nudged me and pointed to Nana's bed. Her arms shot out from under the blanket. She sat up on the side of the bed, groggy and rubbing her closed eyes.

"What happened?" Nana yawned. "I feel like a freight train ran over me."

She opened her eyes, and I fell back against Paul.

One of her hazel eyes was bright blue. Just like Paul's.

CHAPTER 21

ALL THAT GLITTERS

Nana noticed the way that Paul and I were staring. "What are you two looking at? You look like you saw a ghost. What happened to all those birds?"

"Paul sucked them into the shell." I wasn't going to lie. Besides, we had to tell her what had happened to her eye.

Nana rubbed her blue eye. "My eye is burning."

I took Paul's hand and squeezed it. "Nana. We have to tell you something."

"What is it?" She got up and stumbled toward the bathroom. "I wonder if I brought any eye drops?"

I let go of Paul and jumped off the bed to intercept her before she reached the bathroom. "Nana, sit down. I'll get you some drops."

"Nonsense." She pushed me aside. "I'm not an invalid. Besides, I need to use the bathroom."

She breezed past me and slammed the door. I looked at Paul and shook my head. I heard the toilet flush, and then the faucet ran.

A high-pitched scream echoed from behind the door. It flew open, and Nana exploded out of the bathroom. "My eye. My eye . . ." She grabbed my shoulders and put her face in mine. "Look at my eye."

"That's what I was trying to tell you," I said.

"That my eye turned blue? She let go of me and turned to Paul. "How?"

Paul went over to Nana, took her hand, and steered her to the bed. "Sit down. I will explain it."

Paul sat next to her. I came over and sat on her other side and held her hand. It was cold and clammy.

"One of the crows pecked out your eye," he said.

I studied her face for a reaction. "Paul healed the wound with his powers."

Nana raised her hand and traced an outline around the blue eye with a finger. "I don't remember."

I inched closer and put my arm around her shoulders. "Paul erased your memory of the attack. You were hysterical. He was afraid you'd go into shock."

Nana studied Paul. "Thank you for saving my eye. Why did it turn blue?"

He shook his head. "I do not know. After you were attacked, my senses indicated to apply pressure to your wound, and it healed."

Nana rubbed her temple next to the blue eye. "How strange," she mumbled.

There was a rap at the door, and I jumped.

Paul shot off the bed and motioned for us to be quiet. He went to the window, peered out, and unbolted the door. A man in jeans, a white collared shirt, and a brown suede jacket poked his head in the doorway. "Are you folks checking out?" he asked.

Nana stood and went over to the door. "We decided to stay another night. You have my card on file?"

He gazed into Nana's face much longer than seemed polite, then nodded. "Yes, ma'am." He backed away and pulled the door shut.

Paul bolted the door and turned to Nana. "We will stay another night?"

"It's going to be dark soon, and I have a hard time driving at night. We can get some sleep and leave first thing in the morning."

"Are we going back home to the beach?" I asked.

Paul stepped between us. "We are being tracked. To go back to Crescent Cove would bring the wrath of the Bahlari down on the town. We must not lead them there."

"Then where do we go?" I asked.

"East to Arizona," Nana said.

"To my house in Phoenix?"

Nana shook her head. "Something in my mind tells me to go to Flagstaff."

"Why there?" I asked.

Paul crossed his arms and smiled. "She is wise," he said. "We need to avoid big cities, crowds, and places people congregate. We are safer in the open, where we can see the enemy coming."

"Skye, did you bring the shell with you? The one that Paul inhabited?" Nana asked.

"It's in my pack. I always keep it with me."

"Could I see it?"

I took it out of my bag and handed it to Nana.

She reached out, and it exploded into a fiery white-blue light when it touched her hand. I screamed and ran over and knocked the shell out of her hand. It fell on the bed, and the light went out. Trembling, I took Nana's hand and examined her palm and fingers for signs of burns. "Nana, your hand looks normal. I thought it burned you."

Nana blinked. "There was no heat, just that blinding light."

I glanced at Paul. He stood on the other side of the room, watching us.

Nana bent down and reached for the shell, then pulled back. She let her fingers creep back, graze the shell, and pull them away again. Again, going down, her fingers brushed the shell, and it remained still. Finally, she gripped it in her hand and picked it up.

"Nana, I don't think you should," I said.

She put her finger to her lips, motioning me to be silent, and held it out away from her body. Then, deep within the shell, there was a flicker of ruby-red light. It grew and spread, pulsing, getting brighter, and beating faster.

Finally, the entire shell glowed an amethyst purple and throbbed in Nana's hand, but it didn't seem to hurt her.

Nana turned to Paul and held out the pulsing shell. "You're not the only master of these shells."

Paul stepped forward, and a smile played across his face. "You inherited more from me than just a blue eye."

"How did you know . . . ?" I stammered, ". . . that the shell would do that?"

Nana held the pulsing shell up to her eyes. "I sensed it. Something new has entered my mind. Like I'm more connected to the universe."

I inched close to Nana and reached out and touched the shell. Its smooth surface was cool. My fingers closed around it and lifted it from Nana's palm. Clutched in my hand, the pulsating colors changed to emerald. The pace seemed to match the rhythm of my heart.

I looked at Paul. "It did the same thing when I found it on the beach with you inside it."

Nana shot a look at Paul. "Did you know about this power?"

He shook his head. "Only that it was my portal to this planet and, ultimately, my prison."

"But you knew about the dark shell," I said.

Paul came over and lifted the shell from my hand. The light faded, and the shell returned to normal. He held it up for us to see. "It transported my entity, so it carries part of my essence."

"Essence?" I asked.

"You would call it my soul," he replied.

"Then it is a part of you," Nana said.

Paul started pacing, clutching the shell. "It is more complicated than that. The shell, our portal, can be used against us. That is why I dug up the dark shell. It is leverage against the Bahlari that used it to come to this world."

"What kind of leverage?" I asked.

He stopped pacing and fixed me with a stare. "To send them back to hell, where they came from."

Nana stepped forward and pointed at the shell in his hand. "But couldn't that also send you back?"

"Yes. Should the Bahlari get custody of my shell, they could send me back to my planet." Paul tossed the shell onto the bed, and it rolled against a pillow.

I went over and picked it up. "Then why didn't you destroy your shell?"

"The same reason that the Bahlari will not destroy their shells. It is a way back to our world." He slumped over. "I cannot destroy my portal. It was my home while I was buried under the sea. He gazed at the shell in my hand. "Would you burn down your own house?"

I stared down at the shell. I didn't have an answer.

CHAPTER 22

A Change of Heart

We packed up and got on the road by the break of dawn. Feeling half asleep, I told Nana I would drive. I was still worried about her eye, but she insisted it was OK. Paul loaded our baggage in the van, watching for crows, but the parking lot was silent.

Nana figured it would take us about six hours to get to Flagstaff. Outside of Needles, on the Arizona border, we stopped at a truck stop for gas and a bite to eat. I gassed up the van while Nana used the bathroom. Paul stood outside the van surveying the area.

Nana returned just as I put the nozzle back on the pump. After that, it was my turn to use the facilities. I headed across the parking lot to the station.

A man darted out from behind the building. "You're evil!" he shouted, pointing at me. "You brought the alien here!" Some of his teeth were missing.

I backed away. There was something wild in his eyes. He looked to be in his twenties, with matted dark hair and grease stains on his t-shirt and jeans.

He rushed forward, flashing a knife.

"Skye!" Paul shouted, charging my way.

The man kept coming.

"Paul! He's got a knife," I screamed.

The man grabbed me around the neck and pressed the knife against my throat. "They told me to stop you. You have to die."

I swallowed and squirmed under the man's tight embrace.

Paul stood about six feet away, staring at the man. "Put the knife down and release her," he said.

The man clamped my neck tighter and pierced my skin with the blade. His hot foul breath made me gag.

Nana rushed up next to Paul and put her hands on her hips. "Young man, let go of her this minute!"

He lowered the blade and shuffled backward but didn't ease the tight grip on my neck.

"Bitch, you have the evil eye," he spat at Nana.

While the man was occupied with Nana, Paul raced forward and wrestled the knife from the attacker's fist. It bounced on the pavement, and Paul kicked it across the tarmac.

I bolted and ran to Nana, throwing my arms around her. She hugged me close and stroked my hair. "You're OK now," she cooed.

Safe in Nana's arms, I began to cry and giggle hysterically at the same time. "Stop it! Stop this now!"

I repeated in my head. Finally, I gathered up my strength, took a deep breath, and looked around.

Paul had the man's arms locked behind his back. Blood ran down the man's chin. "You dare to defy the Anunnaki," he spat, with his deranged face planted on the asphalt.

Paul jerked the man's arms tight. "Who are the Anunnaki?"

"The underworld gods," he said, grimacing.

"Paul, we have to call the police," I said.

"No police," Paul said. "This man is a pawn, just like the crows." He released his grip on the man and went over and picked up the knife.

"He's right," Nana said. "We're dealing with supernatural forces here. The authorities would never understand."

"Then what do we do?" I said.

The man was picking himself up off the ground.

"Stay down, Mister!" Nana yelled. She went over, kicked the man square in the butt, and he fell on his face.

"We fight," Nana said.

The attacker scrambled back across the pavement on all fours, behind the building from where he came.

Nana cupped her hands around her mouth. "Let those Anunnaki or Bahlari know they've met their match," she shouted after him.

I looked at Nana. "How are we going to fight them? We don't have any weapons."

Nana smiled, "We don't need weapons. We've got the big guns."

"Big guns?" I asked her.

"We've got the shells. I have a feeling they will protect us," Nana said.

We got back in the van and headed toward Flagstaff. Nana drove, and I rode shotgun while Paul got on my cell phone to research the Anunnaki. As the deranged man indicated, the underworld gods were our nemesis.

Paul read us an article he found online. "According to Hopi legend, the Anunnaki or Ant People were vital to the survival of the Hopi. During two global catastrophes, the Ant People led the Hopi to underground caverns in the Grand Canyon. There, they taught the Hopi ancestors how to survive underground by growing food and building dwellings in the rocks."

Nana locked eyes with Paul through the rearview mirror. "It sounds like the Anunnaki are a benevolent race. What would they have in common with the Bahlari?"

Paul leaned forward and squeezed Nana's shoulder. "We must go and check out the Grand Canyon and find out if there is a connection."

I sucked in my breath, waiting for Nana to challenge Paul's decision.

Nana looked back at him and nodded her head. We were on our way.

The VW van pulled into the Grand Canyon campground just before sunset. Nana threw open the door and bolted to the tiny restroom sitting under a huge ponderosa pine. Paul stretched his muscles while I dug out a water bottle from the ice chest.

We had stopped in Williams, Arizona, for camping supplies. Paul and I threw a tarp on the ground and set up the tent. The instructions were impossible to read, but we got it right after a few miserable tries. We loaded our sleeping bags inside while Nana lit the propane stove and boiled some rice. She threw in a couple of cans of chicken soup and buttered up some slices of bread from a French baguette she had picked up at the store. I was so hungry I couldn't remember the last time I'd had a better meal.

After supper, while Nana and I cleaned up, Paul gathered wood for a fire. I showed him how to stack the branches and added some pinecones to fuel the flames. Then we grabbed our folding camp chairs from the van and sat around the campfire. A cool breeze rustled through the pines, reminding me of the sound of the ocean.

Nana leaned toward Paul. "Now that we're here, what are your plans?"

He threw his hands behind his neck and leaned back against the canvas. "There are more Bahlari shells down in the Grand Canyon. I have got to find them. I will start at dawn and search the canyon. You both stay here and wait for my return."

I sat forward in my chair. "Oh, no. I'm going with you."

"It is too dangerous. The Bahlari instill fear and feed off the fright that the person generates. My mind can counteract their torment. You would be defenseless. I will not subject you to their torture."

I shook my head. "Being with you has already put us in danger. What's the difference if it's here or down there?"

"She's right," Nana said. "I'd go too, but I'm not sure I could make the climb back up."

I crossed my arms over my chest. "Then it's settled. We leave in the morning."

"Wait!" Nana sat forward. "You need a permit to hike down the Canyon. People sometimes wait a year to get one."

"No problem." Paul smiled. "If someone approaches me for one, I will use my power of persuasion to convince them I have a permit."

Nana laughed. "The perks of knowing an alien."

We sat around enjoying the fire. It wasn't long before a group of elk grazed around our campsite. Paul got up and approached an enormous ten-point buck.

"Be careful. They can be dangerous," I called.

He looked at me and smiled. "These docile beasts know they can trust me," he said, reaching out and stroking the buck between his eyes. The creature lowered its head, enjoying the attention.

Nana hefted herself out of her chair and went to a nearby doe. She reached out and stroked her on the head. The elk pushed her forehead against Nana's fluttering hand. I got up and went over to touch the elk Nana was petting. I reached out, and the startled animal darted into the brush.

I frowned. "Apparently, I don't have the magic touch you both have."

Paul laughed. "Now that Nana has the alien eye, there is no telling what she can do."

"It doesn't seem fair that I'm the only one without powers," I pouted.

Paul came over and put his arm around me. "Nana paid a high price for her powers," he whispered. "She lost an eye."

I leaned into his strong shoulder and winced. "I'm sorry. That was childish of me. I was just feeling left out."

He wrapped his arm around me and pulled me closer. "You have your own special magic. After all, how many girls are fortunate enough to find an alien in a seashell?"

I turned to him and smiled. "You always have the answer to everything. No wonder the girls find you so attractive." I leaned in and brushed my lips against his.

"Hey, you two," Nana called. "We better get to bed. You have a long day ahead tomorrow."

"Yes, ma'am!" I smiled and saluted.

Nana went to the van while Paul and I opened our sleeping bags in the tent.

It was getting chilly, so I climbed into my bag wearing sweats. Paul reached over and turned off the lantern.

I lay in the dark, listening to Paul's shallow breathing, wondering if he was asleep.

"You awake?" I whispered.

"Yes." He rolled toward me.

"I was just wondering if Nana will be OK here by herself. Do you think she could be in any danger?"

"The Bahlari are more interested in me and what I will find in the Canyon. That is why you should stay here with her. It would be safer for you."

"And worry about you the whole time? No way."

I closed my eyes and dreamed of standing on a ledge that hung over the Grand Canyon. "Come on down into the canyon," a musical voice called from below. Then, soft against the breeze and rustling pines, another voice. "Come down the trail, a path you'll soon know well."

Suddenly, a chorus of singing voices rose from where I stood. "Come down to the Canyon, hurry, don't delay. Come down, and see the price you'll pay!"

I woke up sweating. Paul must have sensed something wasn't right. He crawled out of his sleeping bag and wiped my brow. "Are you all right?"

"I had a dream. Voices were calling me to come down into the Canyon."

"The Bahlari," Paul said.

"Why are they calling me?"

"To frighten you. To feed off your fear. It will be sunrise soon. We should get ready to go."

When we climbed out of the tent, Nana was lighting the stove to make coffee.

"Did you get up to see us off?" I asked her.

"See you off?" Nana straightened up and put her hands on her hips. "Bullshit! I'm going with you."

"But you said you couldn't make it back up the canyon?"

Paul stepped forward. "If you cannot keep up, you will slow us down."

"If this new blue eye's powers don't help, I'll spring for a helicopter ride back up. There's no way I'm staying here while you two are down there fighting God knows what."

"I cannot let you take that chance. You might die down there," Paul said.

"It's my life, not yours. I've made up my mind. You can't stop me." Nana crossed her arms and gave an icy stare, daring us to challenge her decision.

"She's right," I said. "Three is better than two. We don't know the extent of Nana's powers, but maybe she can help us."

Paul shook his head in defeat, knowing he was outnumbered. "Then we better get ready to go; it will be light soon."

We spread our provisions on a blanket and carefully packed what we thought we would need into full-size overnight backpacks. We let Nana take a light daypack. Paul was willing to carry the extra weight of two sleeping bags and a small tent for Nana and me. We packed plenty of water, knowing we wouldn't find any until we reached the bottom of the canyon.

All loaded up, we started out at first light. We walked about a mile from the campground, and the canyon rim loomed ahead.

We reached the rim at sunrise. The view was breathtaking; I stood in awe of its beauty. I'd lived in Phoenix my whole life, but never had the opportunity to visit the Canyon.

"Oh, my," Nana gasped. "I was here many years ago but had forgotten this place's majesty and power."

Paul took my hand. "The canyon is amazing."

Several crows squawking in a nearby pinion pine broke the silence. Paul let go of my hand, picked up a rock, and heaved it into the branches. The hideous birds took flight, dropping shit bombs over our heads. I screamed and threw my jacket up over my hair.

"Do not panic," Paul called out. "That is what the Bahlari want."

"Get the hell out of here," Nana yelled at the crows.

I started running. "Let's get moving before something worse attacks us."

We started down the steep track single file. Paul led, and Nana trailed behind me. When we stopped to rest a few hundred feet below, there were cliffs and terraces, walls of colors beyond anything I could have imagined. Embedded in the ancient rock were layers of reds, pinks, purples, and every other color of the rainbow, reminding me of the colors of Paul's shell, only on a grander scale.

Gazing up from where we had just started and then into the depths below, I wondered if it was physically possible for Nana to make the trek. I turned and looked back at Nana trailing behind.

Nana caught my eye and winked. "Penny, for your thoughts," she said.

Embarrassed, I looked away. Could she know what I was thinking?

CHAPTER 23

EDGE OF THE WORLD

We stood at the edge of a precipice. Thousands of feet below, a great valley spread before our eyes. Far across, the distant mountains were covered in shades of purples. The climb down the trail was so gradual that we barely noticed it. It was like looking into a bottomless pit. In the distance, I saw the Colorado River winding along the canyon's bed.

"Look at that view," breathed Nana. "It's like a different world."

Paul came over and stood beside Nana. "The Bahlari lurk somewhere down there," he said.

"It's hard to believe there is evil where there is so much beauty," Nana replied.

"Do you have any idea where the Bahlari are hiding?" I asked.

Paul shook his head. "I am not positive. We will have to go farther down into the canyon to find out."

The trail turned sharply to the left and dropped over the edge as a faintly marked footpath zigzagged down the almost vertical face.

"From the number of footprints, it looks like a few creatures have gone up and down here," Nana said as she looked over the edge of the dizzying trail.

"We had better head back and look for an easier way down," Paul suggested.

"No," Nana said. "If something has gone up and down this way, we can too."

Knowing about my fear of heights, Paul raised an eyebrow. "What do you want to do, Skye?"

I'd volunteered for this adventure, knowing full well that there would be obstacles. If Nana could do it, then so could I. I looked back at him and shrugged my shoulders. "Count me in."

"Take my hands, both of you; it is very steep," he said.

We started down the sheer path. Paul had a tight grip on us, but the descent was exhausting. Sometimes, it seemed impossible to go on, but climbing back up would have been too hard.

Nana slipped on more than one occasion, and each time Paul caught her before she plummeted over the cliff. She joked, making light of her clumsiness. I admired her bravery.

We stopped to rest on some flat boulders along the side of the trail. I heard a noise below and looked over the cliff. A lizard about ten feet long was climbing sluggishly up toward us. The creepy thing was covered with red, black, and gray scales. It had a head like a crocodile, with two white horns on each side of its jaw.

"What's that?" I screamed.

Nana backed away from the ledge. "I didn't know anything like that existed. It looks dangerous."

"It is one of the Bahlari's minions. More deadly than the crows," Paul replied.

"Climb back out of its way," Paul said. "I will distract it here until you are both safe."

The creature was not aware of our presence, but in another moment, we would cross paths. Paul pried a boulder from the cliff and hurled it down, attempting to turn the creature back. The rock struck it on the snout, and it stopped short, snorted, raised its head, and looked me square in the eye.

Like lightning, it scurried up the steep trail straight in my direction. Before I could get out of its way, a long-forked tongue lashed out, curled around my waist, and snapped me toward its gaping jaws.

My mouth opened, and I heard my strangled screams wailing off the canyon walls. I pounded on its ugly head with my fists to keep from being its next meal.

A foul odor escaped its hideous mouth, and I felt myself growing dizzy. Before I knew it, Nana was at my side.

Nana lunged at the beast, beating it with her fists to keep its jaws away from me. She was risking her life to save me, but where was Paul?

"Run, Nana!" I cried. "Run, or it will kill us both."

Ignoring my warnings, she continued to pound the beast with her fists again and again.

Paul ran out of the brush holding a long pointed branch. He hefted the makeshift spear and plunged it into the creature's eye. The reptile turned on Paul with a high-pitched scream and tried to strike him with its sharp horns. Paul stood his ground and drove the weapon deep into the other eye, thrusting again and again.

As the point of the spear pierced its brain, the creature went limp, and I fell from its grasp to the ground.

I jumped up, threw my arms around Paul, buried my face in his chest, and held him tight.

After a few moments in Paul's arms, my heart stopped racing. Finally, I let go and turned to Nana. "Thank you," I said. "You risked your life to save me."

"I was afraid I would lose you," she said.

"We had better be on our guard. There might be more of those creatures lurking around," Paul said.

"Look down there," I pointed to a spring running out between the rocks below. "I would love to wash up and have a drink."

"We will head to the water," Paul said. "Then, I will scout for branches to sharpen into spears in case one of those creatures attacks again."

We started the descent, and I picked up the pace, my eagerness for the cool spring growing with every step. Finally, I rounded a cluster of red rocks that made up the face of the cliff we were scaling. We were only about twenty feet above the ground, but the trail had become an almost vertical drop.

Paul pushed me into a recess between the rocks. "Wait here. I will help Nana down and come back for you." He turned to Nana and crouched down. "Get on my back and hold on tight."

Nana threw her hands on her hips. "You've got to be kidding. You can't carry me. I'm twice your weight. We'll figure out another way down."

Paul wiped his brow and flashed a smile. "Do you not have faith in my abilities? I will get you and Skye down safely."

Nana shook her head. "We'll end up in a heap in the rocks below if you try to carry me down."

"Paul saved me from the riptide. He has superhuman powers," I said.

Paul bent down, and Nana reluctantly pressed against his back and put her arms around his neck. "OK, you win, but superpowers or not, it will be like hauling a beached whale."

Paul laughed. "Stay close to the rocks and wait for me to come back, Skye."

He started down the cliff, digging his hands into the cracks in the boulders while Nana balanced precariously on his back with her eyes tightly shut.

It wasn't long before Paul brought Nana safely to the ground and was on his way back for me. I climbed on his back and shut my eyes. Before I knew it, we were down. Somewhere nearby, I heard the bubbling of a stream. The gurgling water reminded me of how hot and thirsty I was. I rushed toward the sound. Sunlight bounced off a small stream hidden by the underbrush.

"Hurry, there's a stream behind the bushes," I called out.

I foraged through the soft vegetation until I reached the shimmering water and collapsed onto my knees in the meadow. Dipping my hand in the water, I brought it to my lips. Cool—so cool, better than anything I had ever tasted. I bent down, lowered my head into the running stream, and drank. I let the water caress my lips like a lover's kiss.

Pulling my face from the water, I rolled onto my back in the low grass. Sunlight twinkled and bounced off boulders that lined the stream. It felt like paradise, and I could have stayed there the rest of the day.

Suddenly, the sky darkened, and I caught my breath as a cloud covered the sun. Dead branches snapped from the trees, and black crows flew overhead.

In the distance, Nana screamed. "Skye, get undercover!"

CHAPTER 24

CALL OF THE WILD

A cloud of crows, squalling and cawing, darkened the sky. Paul ran up and put his arm around me, and we ran to join Nana under a cluster of trees. The air was hot and humid. The sun shone off their silky oily feathers while they uttered hoarse ugly cries. I could see the rage in their beady black eyes; they were ready to peck us to death. Were crows meat-eaters? They must be. They'd gone after Nana's eye.

The squawks of the pursuing crows grew fainter. I knew they hadn't followed us into the cover of trees. Soon, off in the distance, I saw the flock disappear around the point of a jagged rock formation.

Moments later, we heard the howling of a wolf.

"Now what?" Nana said. "I thought all the wolves in Arizona were extinct."

I frowned. "I never knew anything like that giant lizard existed either," I said.

"It must be more of the Bahlari's minions," Paul said.

More howling joined the lone cry of the wolf. Then, with no warning, two wolves ran out from the brush and circled around us.

"Paul!" Nana shrieked as a wolf leapt at him.

Paul whipped around with the sharpened spear in his hand to strike the beast, but it knocked him down before he could lash out. The wolf's jaws strained for Paul's throat, but its jaws clamped on the spear he threw up to protect his face.

Nana and I rushed to help Paul. I slammed the animal in the head with my pack, and Nana kicked it in its side. The wolf yelped, released the stick, and snapped at Nana's foot. She kicked it in the snout, which drove the animal into a frenzy.

The wolf backed up, growled at Nana, and leaped.

An explosion rang in my ear. I watched the wolf sail past Nana and land on the ground, blood and guts surrounding its body. The other wolf ran off into the underbrush.

"What happened?" I looked around but saw no one.

Paul jumped up off the ground. "Someone fired a weapon at the wolf. I wonder where they went?"

"Do you think the wolves will come back?"

"I do not know," he said. "The Bahlari sent these creatures, so they know we are here."

"Then let's move on," Nana said. "It's better than staying here being sitting ducks."

We hoisted our packs and started across an overgrown trail that scaled the face of a cliff several hundred feet high on one side. The other side dropped off a few hundred feet to the bottom of a rocky ravine. I sucked in my breath and hugged the cliffside as we hiked across the path.

My senses were on high alert, between the steep ravine and my fear of running into another of those giant lizards. Soon the trail widened, and we came to the entrance of a vast cave in the canyon wall.

A young couple dressed in ordinary jeans and t-shirts emerged from the cave. They wore backpacks and carried rifles. The man had close-cropped black hair, an olive complexion, and hard muscles. The woman had high cheekbones, a chiseled nose, and long silky black hair that flowed loosely around her thin but muscled frame. She matched the man in height. Probably a couple of hikers exploring the wilderness. I wondered if they were the ones who had shot the wolf.

As they got closer, a chill ran down my spine. Their eyes were blue, like Paul's.

Paul stepped forward. "Did you shoot the wolf that attacked us?" There was curiosity in his voice.

"I shot it," the woman said. She approached Paul, reached out, and touched his cheek, studying him. "You have the eyes of a convert."

Paul stood still and let the woman probe his features. Nana and I exchanged a surprised look at the interaction.

"A convert?" Paul asked.

"A spirit that inhabits the body of one who is no longer conscious," the man said. His eyes flickered to me, then back to Paul.

He turned to Nana. "The old woman has one convert eye."

Nana's nostrils flared. "Who are you calling an old woman? I can run circles around you any day of the week!"

"That's right. She made it down here," I said, daring him to contradict me.

"It seems we got off on the wrong start," the woman said. "I am Tansy, and he is Kitori. We are guardians of the cave."

"Guardians of the cave?" I asked.

Paul stepped forward. "You are of my species. Why do you guard this cave?"

"Inside the cave is a subterranean hole in the Earth. It is called Sipapuni, the emergence place of our adopted people, the Hopi," said Kitori. "Inside, our ancestors were fed and clothed by the Ant People, extraterrestrials that could not survive on the surface of the Earth."

"Why did you come to the surface if aliens cared for you?" Nana asked.

"Our goddess, Spider Woman, ordered our ancestors to ascend to the surface," Tansy said.

"Is that why you guard the cave?" Paul repeated.

"We guard it because of an invasion by the Bahlari."

"Why would the Bahlari want to invade the cave?" Paul asked.

"The Bahlari cannot tolerate sunlight," Kitori replied. "They invaded the caves and drove out the Ant People."

"Why would the Bahlari want to stay on this planet and live subterranean? What was their purpose? It sounds like a dull existence," Nana said.

"The Earth, manipulated by the Bahlari, is a place of suffering," Kitori replied. People are betrayed, cheated, killed, slaughtered, raped, and tortured. As a result, disease and famine are widespread. In addition, the pollution caused by humankind is killing off animal and sea life."

"Why would the Bahlari choose to destroy the world they live in?" Nana asked.

"The Bahlari feed on violence and negative emotions," Tansy said. "They generate war and dissension in humans and access the energy that creates. Rage, fear, hate, panic, and lust are negative emotions they crave. The more a victim suffers, the more adverse energy is released for them to absorb."

"When the Bahlari came to Earth thousands of years ago, they could not bring their technology with them through the portal," Kitori said. "But in the last century, humans have advanced, making it possible for the Bahlari to access mass weapons of destruction. As a result, they are planning to cause another World War. If they have their way, it will end humanity."

"If that's true," Nana said, "then they will destroy themselves along with everyone else."

"Not so, Grandmother. They will move on to another world and start their reign of destruction again," Kitori told her.

"Please, call me Nana." She smiled, but it didn't reach her eyes.

Kitori bowed his head. "Nana."

Since it seemed time for introductions, I stepped forward. "I'm Skye, and this is Paul."

Kitori nodded at me and turned to Paul. "You have the eyes of a new entity. Deep and strong."

Tansy looked intrigued. "I noticed it the moment I looked at his face," she said.

"I am a first-generation convert, as you call it," Paul said.

"How can that be?" Kitori said.

"Where have you been?" Tansy asked.

Paul told them how he had been trapped under the ocean floor in the shell. I explained what happened after I found him and put him in human Paul's brain when he was in the coma.

Tansy moved to Paul and gently touched his face again, studying his eyes. "Your powers are strong. Kitori and I have transcended a few generations, moving from body to body. It has drained our resources. You are new and strong. We need you to join us in the fight against the Bahlari."

"We will provide safe passage for the girl and Nana back up the canyon. There is no place for them here," Kitori said.

"I'm not leaving," I said, standing tall.

Nana folded her arms across her chest. "Me, either."

"I will join you in fighting the Bahlari, but we all stay together. We have come this far together and will continue with or without your help," Paul said.

I smiled at Nana, and she grinned back. I didn't like the way Tansy had caressed Paul's face. There was no way I was leaving them alone, fight or no fight.

"All they can do is get in the way!" Kitori protested. "An old woman and human girl will only slow us down."

"Now listen, Buster." Nana raised her fist. "I told you not to call me that. This is the last time I'm putting up with your crap."

Kitori frowned and kicked at the dirt with his boot. "What are you going to do? Beat me up?"

Tansy stepped forward. "Knock it off, Kitori. This is serious business. We need Paul's help in our battle with the Bahlari."

"At least the girl is young and strong," Kitori said. "Cyclopes Nana will only get in our way."

"All right. I warned you." Nana stormed over, grabbed Kitori's ear, and yanked his head to her lips. "Young man, didn't your momma teach you any manners?"

Kitori twisted and pulled loose of Nana's grip. "I never knew my mother," he spat. "This body was implanted with my entity. Tansy and I have gone through several host bodies in the past hundred years."

"I'm sorry to hear that," Nana said. "But it gives you no right to disrespect your elders."

Kitori laughed. "Lady, I am much older than you. You should be showing me some respect."

Paul looked annoyed. "Nana has her own powers," he interrupted. "When the crows pecked out her eye, I reinserted it. As a result, she possesses a fragment of my entity."

"What can the power of one eye do against the Bahlari?" Kitori said.

Nana fumbled inside her pack. She pulled a bundle out wrapped in a blanket and laid it on the ground at Kitori's feet. "I might not be as powerful as the Bahlari," Nana said as she hunched down and unwrapped two conch shells, one light, the other dark. She stood with a shell clutched in each fist and raised them toward Kitori. "But I also have weapons of mass destruction."

·· 🐚 ··

CHAPTER 25

THE SHELL GAME

The shocked look on their faces made me wonder why the shells could have scared them that much. Tansy gripped Kitori's arm and held him like she was about to pass out. The shells that Nana held out affected them deeply.

"Tansy, they have the Bahlari's shell!" Kitori exclaimed.

"The dark one is a Bahlari's portal into this world," Paul agreed.

"What about the other one?" Tansy said.

"It was my portal. The shell Skye found me in before my conversion. Like us, the Bahlari used the shells as a portal to get to this planet," Paul said.

Tansy stepped forward. "We need to show you something."

"What are you doing?" Kitori said, grabbing Tansy by the arm.

Tansy pulled away from him. "We need his advice," she said, pointing at Paul.

"Bring the convert only. The others can wait here," Kitori said.

"We stay together," Paul declared.

Kitori and Tansy exchanged looks. Their eyes, although much like Paul's, were not as deep blue.

Tansy pointed to the cave. "Then follow us."

"Can we trust them?" Nana said. "It might be a trap to lock us in the cave."

"They are of my race," Paul said. "I trust they intend to protect Earth from the Bahlari."

"We shot the wolf that attacked you," Tansy said.

"Then why didn't you stay and introduce yourselves?" Nana said.

Kitori pointed at Paul. "We didn't realize he was one of us until we saw his eyes. We shy away from humans, so we don't draw attention to ourselves and the cave."

"Then why did you shoot the wolf?" I asked.

"We don't want to see anyone hurt," Tansy said. "We have a duty to protect humans."

"Why is that?" Nana said.

"The Hopi have protected our entities since we arrived on Earth," Kitori said. "They are our family."

Nana clapped her hands. "Well, it's settled. They saved us, so I guess I can trust them."

Nana replaced the shells in her pack and we followed them into the mouth of the cave. About twenty feet inside was a metal grate with a lock. Tansy unclipped a ring of keys from her belt and unlocked the gate. It opened with a screech. She motioned us through, then slammed it shut and locked it behind her.

Nana tapped Tansy on the shoulder. "Can't you leave the door unlocked?

Tansy shook her head. "We cannot take the chance of someone wandering in here."

Nana wiped the sweat off her brow. "Just thought I'd ask."

Kitori handed us flashlights from his pack and led us through a dark tunnel barely high enough to stand upright. Nana and I followed Kitori; Paul and Tansy took the rear. The farther we went, the narrower the tunnel became. After a few hundred feet, we dropped to our knees and crawled into the darkness.

A whiff of sulfurous air, like rotten eggs, filled the air. "It smells toxic in here. Are you sure it's safe?" I shouted.

"Sorry, I farted," Nana replied. "I'm claustrophobic. That's what happens when I get nervous."

We started up a rocky path and squeezed under an overhang at the top. It opened into a cavern with a smooth sandstone floor. The room was long and narrow, and we could stand. At the end of the room was another tunnel. Kitori motioned us to follow him.

Once inside, this tunnel ended in solid rock and a massive wooden door inscribed with hieroglyphics. It looked ancient but was perfectly preserved, protected by that dark, dry place where sunlight couldn't penetrate.

Paul stepped forward and traced the symbols etched on the door with his finger.

"Do you sense anything?" I asked.

"I do not recognize these symbols," Paul answered.

"They are the writings of the ancient ones, our people of long ago," Kitori said.

Tansy fished through her collection of keys and produced a golden skeleton key from the ring. She inserted it into the lock, turned it to the right, and the door slid open.

"It appears you're the custodian of the keys," Nana said.

Tansy smiled. "It is my destiny."

She pulled the heavy door back, and we followed her inside. The bright light behind the door blinded me after being in the dark tunnel. I closed my eyes to let them get adjusted to the light.

When I opened my eyes, I saw an enormous cavern about ten stories high, lit by various openings in the ceiling. Sunlight reflected off the hanging stalactites and gleamed off stalagmites rising from the floor.

"Oh, my God," Nana whispered as we wandered through a narrow, winding trail between the massive stalagmites. A ribbon of water cascading down the red rock wall emptied into a clear stream, cutting a path through the sandstone floor. Numerous tunnels branched off on either side of the cavern.

"Where do those tunnels go?" I asked.

"They are entrances to a vast underground network of tunnels used by the Ant People long ago," Kitori answered.

As we advanced farther, a series of cliff-dwelling rooms made of mud and logs lined the upper reaches of the ceiling. They reminded me of the sandcastles I'd built on the beach back at Nana's when I was a kid. I turned to Kitori, puzzled. "What are cliff dwellings doing inside the cave?"

Kitori pointed up to them. "These were built before our ancient people ascended to the surface," he said. "For many years, sentries that guarded the Bahlari used these dwellings as their homes."

"How did they keep the Bahlari from escaping?" Nana asked.

"The Bahlari are extraterrestrials," Kitori said, "but they are restricted to living underground in the enormous ancient caverns and tunnel complexes. They are sensitive to the sunlight, so they remain subterranean, but they control an ancient secret global social network above."

"The government, the CIA, and NSA must know about them," Nana said.

"There has been a massive cover-up by certain global money and religious powers of the existence of the Bahlari," Tansy told her. "For centuries, the Vatican has been aware of their presence."

"These people and organizations in power," Kitori said, "traded knowledge and wealth for the murder and torture of common citizens. The Bahlari, in turn, fed off their fear; it sustains them."

Nana looked cross. "Why do the people in power protect them?"

"Because they feed knowledge and power to the chosen few who run the world," Kitori said.

"After all this time, it's strange that no one's ever reported them to the media?" I asked.

"Stories and articles appear along the way, but they are usually disregarded as conspiracy theories," Tansy answered. "But in 1909," she continued, "an archeologist stumbled upon this cavern and removed hundreds of ancient artifacts. They ended up in the Smithsonian Institute, but the higher powers covered up the find. They would have stayed hidden if not for an article in the *Arizona Gazette* in April 1909, which stated that the artifacts were found in the underground world where the Hopi originated and were fed and clothed by the Ant People."

"Ever since that article," Kitori continued, "they beefed up security to ensure no one else violated our sacred land at the bottom of the canyon."

"What happened to the Ant People? "Nana asked.

"They are the aliens some people call the Greys," Kitori said. "Those described with big black oval eyes and large heads. They were expelled down here by the Bahlari but still have a presence on Earth. We don't understand their agenda, but they did take care of our people below. They have never given us reason to believe they are dangerous or mean us harm."

"Wow," Nana said. "We hit the alien jackpot. The Bahlari, the Greys, and you two and Paul. Are there any more running around?"

"There were twelve of us, so nine others might be somewhere out there," Tansy told her. "We don't know how many remain. The portals were scattered across the Earth when we emerged, and we lost touch over the years."

Paul was quietly taking in everything that was being said.

"If the Bahlari are trapped below because they can't live on the surface, why do you need to post guards for them?" I asked.

"They might be able to walk the Earth at night," Kitori answered. "There have been rumors of that happening in the past."

"With today's technology," Tansy said, "we had the tools to seal the Bahlari below. That is why only the two of us guard the entrance."

"What technology do you use to keep them confined underground?" Paul asked.

"Come with us," Kitori answered. "We will show you."

A four-wheel ATV side by side sat against a tunnel at the cavern's far wall. Kitori got in the driver's seat, and Tansy rode shotgun. I squeezed in the back between Paul and Nana. Kitori fired up the engine, and we took off. Inside the tunnel, glowing lights lined the path. We descended so fast that I pushed against the front seat and fought to keep my balance.

After about a mile or so, we drove into another sizable cavern lit by floodlights that circled the cave's ceiling. The ATV came to a stop, and Kitori and Tansy jumped out of the vehicle, followed by the three of us.

Nana slapped my shoulder with her mouth open. "Look at that!"

A glass dome covered a pit that opened half a block into the earth. Underneath, the gaping hole went down farther than the lights above could reach. I went cold, wondering if any human being had ever descended into this yawning black hole and lived to tell about it.

I turned to Paul. "It feels like you could lose your soul in this pit."

He nodded. "The entrance to the Bahlari's subterranean caverns." Paul turned to Kitori. "Is that how you've kept them contained?"

"We installed the dome to imprison the Bahlari and to keep strangers out of the caves."

"Once word got out that this site was here back in 1909, we had to ensure this trench was not disturbed again," Tansy agreed. "The archeologists who raided the caverns took some artifacts, but our people were able to retrieve them after negotiations with the Smithsonian."

Nana reached into her pack and drew out the dark shell. "I wonder if they found any more of these down there." She waved the shell in the air over the dome as she spoke.

The cave suddenly trembled.

A fissure cracked in the sandstone floor. The lights flickered and came back on, and a noise like howling wind blew up through the crack. After that, the lights got brighter and brighter. We covered our eyes with our hands to keep from being blinded.

Suddenly, the entire cave shifted to one side, and I fell against Nana and Paul. Chunks of rock and debris rained down from the ceiling. We covered our heads with our hands as the stones pelted our heads and shoulders.

A crack appeared in the dome, and I could smell hot steam escaping from underneath into the air. The stench from the escaping vapor was so pungent that I gagged.

"Paul, what's happening?" I screamed.

"The introduction of the new Bahlari shell must have awakened something below," he said.

"And boy, are they pissed," Nana added through clenched teeth.

The shaking in the cave stopped. Then, a noise like a runaway train echoed through the cavern. Next, the lights went out.

Goosebumps broke out on my arms, and a deep chill went through my body. Something bad was about to happen. Something very bad. I wrapped my arms around my chest to warm myself, but it didn't help. My body felt frozen. Finally, I opened my mouth to warn Nana and Paul.

"Watch out!" I screamed into the darkness.

CHAPTER 26

DARKNESS FALLS

A wet smell of steam assaulted my nose as I lay curled on my side in the dark. Hot, stifling air filled my lungs, stealing my breath as it gripped my throat. *I can't breathe! I can't breathe!* I clenched my teeth until, at last, my tortured lungs gasped scorched air. I drifted in and out of consciousness. The loud noise and motion of the cave had subsided. It was silent. I tried calling out to Paul and Nana, but words barely escaped my lips. I felt so alone, lying in the dark and wondering if the rumbling would start again.

"Is anyone there?" I groaned. "Nana? Paul? Are you alright? Can you hear me?"

I tried to push up, but my sore shoulders screamed with pain, my elbow gave way, and I collapsed onto my back. Get up, get moving, I thought and righted myself.

Crawling on the ground like a crab, I felt around for something familiar. I tried to stand, but the thick smoke in the air drove me back to the ground. Was I the only one alive in here? The thought of being trapped in here alone sent shivers down my spine. I knew I could never find my way out of here by myself.

A shriek from the darkness to my left brought me out of my daze. I whirled to face the noise, and the screech became the shrill wail of a beast. A pair of hungry eyes glowed in the dark. I threw my arms up to protect my face and screamed again. Finally, the eyes retreated into the blackness.

"Skye," Paul coughed out.

"Oh, thank God," I shrieked. "Paul, there's some kind of creature in here. I think I scared it off, but it's so dark I can't see. Where are you?"

"North of you," he said. "Nana has had an accident. She is unconscious. Her head is bleeding, but she is breathing. Can you make your way over to us? I do not want to leave her alone."

"Keep talking, and I'll follow your voice," I said.

"What should I say?"

"Tell me a story." I would have asked him to sing, but I didn't think he knew any songs.

"We came to this planet because the Bahlari attacked our world. They thought they could feed off our fear and corrupt us as they did to this world and many others."

I homed in on his monotonous tone and crawled toward him and Nana through the darkness. "Keep talking," I shouted.

My legs were stiff, and I stumbled over debris and broken pieces of machinery. Finally, I paused, took several deep breaths to keep from passing out, and went on, feeling my way toward Paul's voice and the story he told.

"They did not realize that we were a cooperative race and had no fear of being corrupted. Since they feed off fear and corruption, it angered them that we could not be tainted."

"Keep talking. I'm almost there," I cried.

"They sent weapons of destruction to our world and began destroying our cities. We fought back and drove them from our planet. That was when we decided to send scouts to fight the Bahlari and their evil reign of terror over other worlds."

Reaching out, I touched Paul's foot. He grabbed my hand and pulled me into his arms. I snuggled in his embrace and kissed his lips. It felt safe to be wrapped in his arms, protected, and no longer alone.

Pulling away, I felt around and touched Nana's body. Her chest rose and fell in a steady rhythm. My hand felt her face; her brow was cool. Blood was dripping from her temple. She must have bumped it during the explosion.

I wiped the blood on my pants and squeezed Paul's hand. "She must have a concussion."

"I scanned her brain, and it is not damaged. She should wake up soon."

I opened my mouth in surprise. "How did you scan her brain? Is that another one of your special powers?"

"It is because she has part of my entity in her eye. So, like you, we are connected."

"One big family," I replied. As soon as the words were out of my mouth, I realized how true this was. Paul and Nana were my only family; without them, I would truly be alone.

"Do you know what happened to Kitori and Tansy?"

"I saw them running for the tunnels as the lights went out."

"How will we get out of here when we can't see in the dark?"

"I need to find my shell. Nana had it before the lights went off."

I felt near the floor by Nana and came across her backpack. My fingers found the zipper. I yanked it open, reached inside, and went through her belongings until I touched the familiar shape. Then, pulling it out, I felt for Paul's hand and passed it to him.

As soon as he grabbed the shell, it glowed like a nightlight, lighting up his dark hair and blue eyes. We stared at each other for a few seconds.

"Bring the shell over to Nana so I can check her injury," I said.

I pulled a bandana and water bottle out of her pack to wipe the blood from around Nana's ear. As I cleaned the wound, her body twisted and contorted. She struggled for a breath, gasping and sputtering. I unzipped her jacket to give her room to breathe and tucked the pack under her head for a pillow.

I eyed Paul. "I don't know what I'll do if she dies."

Paul reached over and brushed my cheek with his fingers. "She is resilient."

I pulled back from his touch. "You don't have to appease me. I'm not a little girl anymore."

"What happened?" Nana muttered.

"Oh, Nana!" I covered her hand with mine and squeezed it. "You fell and bumped your head when the lights went out."

Nana fought to raise her head and collapsed back against the pack. "I feel so weak." Her eyes moved toward the shell. "Can I hold it?" she asked.

Paul held out the glowing object and her fingers curled around the shell. "Oh," Nana said. "Touching this makes me feel good." She ran her fingers over the shell's ridges with a need in her eyes. "The colors are so beautiful," she whispered.

The shell pulsated brighter, and the light intensified as Nana stroked its outer casing. Soon, the glow lit up the entire cave as Nana's beaming eyes caressed the shell like a long-lost lover. Around and around, the colors danced across the rocks and walls of the cavern.

Suddenly, the shell flared like the sun, and the cave lit up like a million candles, blinding me for a few moments. When the flare subsided, the shell lit the chamber as if the lights had never gone out. Then, the clean, fresh aroma of a pine forest replaced the air's hot, dank, wet smell. I inhaled the scent into my choked lungs. Was I dreaming?

"It smells like Christmas," I said.

Paul passed his hand over the shell clutched in Nana's palm and looked into her eyes. "You have a gift. An understanding of the powers of the shell."

Nana stared back at Paul. "Then I must have inherited it from you when you fixed my eye." She handed the shell to Paul and stood. "It's already made me feel better. My understanding of it is limited, but I'm doing my best."

Paul walked around, shining the shell's light over the wall of boulders and slabs, assessing the damage in the cavern. Debris was strewn across the ground, and steam hissed from pipes running against the wall. Fallen boulders completely blocked the entrance to the escape tunnel.

My heart began to race. What if we were trapped? "How are we going to get out of here?" I asked in a shaky voice.

"That's not our biggest problem," Paul answered. "The outer glass seal is broken. The Bahlari could be lurking anywhere."

Nana looked out over the shattered dome. "What the hell just happened?"

CHAPTER 27

HELL HATH NO FURY

Smoke rose from the broken dome, the pine forest smell that the shell created dissipated, and the sulfurous stench became overpowering. My head throbbed from the reek, but that was the least of my problems. Tendrils of cold gripped me when I thought of what could happen. If we didn't find a way out of here soon, I feared the Bahlari would make sure we never got out alive.

I walked through the fog rising from the cracked dome to get closer to it. Then, a hiss of hot steam flew across my face, blinding me. I lost my balance and stumbled, falling onto the dome.

"No! No! No!" I screamed as my body swayed, spinning like a saucer toward the opening in the dome.

Paul ran and jumped on the dome, attempting to stop me from falling into the pit. With super speed, he scrambled after me across the glass, but I shot out of control through the hole before he could reach me. Then, something caught on my jacket, ripping it, and I dangled in midair over the open pit.

I looked up to see Paul's face. He looked worried as he peered over the rim about fifteen feet above. "Skye, hold on, and I will find something to lower down to you to get you up."

Breathless and scared, unable to answer, I gave him a thumbs up. He would find a way to rescue me.

Nana's face peeked over the edge above me. "Hold on, Skye," she called down. "He's found a loose cable to use to get you back up here."

A steel cable snaked over the rim toward my dangling body. I reached out, grabbed the swinging line, and clenched it in my damp palms. "Got it," I called up to Paul. I unhooked my jacket from the metal debris that had saved me and swung free.

Despite the throbbing in my shoulders and the pain in my arms, I would have to pull myself up the cable line. I placed one hand above the other and pulled upward. The muscles in my shoulder and arm shrieked with pain, and I almost collapsed backward into the abyss.

"I'm too weak to climb the cable," I cried.

Paul's voice echoed back. "Hold on tight, and I will pull you up."

"OK." I caught my breath, fought back the pain, clutched the slippery cable with all my might, brought my knees up, and wrapped my legs around it.

The cable climbed toward the rim, and my hands strained to hold on. The air was hot and stale. I took deep gulps of air to keep from passing out. A gust of hot, bitter wind blew sand in my face, almost knocking me off the cable. My eyes teared against the gritty wind. When my vision cleared, I looked up into the hazy light at the top of the shaft about ten feet above.

"Hurry, Paul!" I don't know how long I can hold on!"

A huge gust of wind blew up from below. The wind shrieked and swirled, spinning me around on the cable. Sparks erupted from the charged air as I fought to hold on to the twisting cable, my only lifeline.

Tears streamed down my cheeks as I lifted my face into the screeching wind. "Paul, please hurry!"

The wind was making the cable swing violently back and forth. Then my shoulder hit an outcrop of rough-edged boulders that lined the wall, knocking the breath out of me. I looked up but couldn't see Paul or Nana, only the cable hanging over the rim.

Five more feet . . . lightning flashed, and part of the dome exploded in a dazzling burst of white, then it faded into a glow like hot coals simmering in the bottom of a BBQ pit.

The cable broke away from the dome's rim. In terrible slow motion, I felt my body being dropped back into the abyss. I felt that everything I loved would be gone and destroyed, even if I survived the fall.

Once my screaming started, it wouldn't stop.

CHAPTER 28

SNAP . . . CRACKLE . . . POP!

Fortunately, I hadn't dropped very far. I got a slanted view of a chute in the wall. Inching over, I sat down hard and slid down the smooth channel that was like a giant slide at a water park. I landed in a pile of rubble at the bottom of a gorge.

What had happened to Paul and Nana? I could see the glow of light up on the dome's rim. Massive pieces of debris hung dangerously off the platform over my head. I moved away to a safer place, under an outcropping of rocks.

I called out for Nana and Paul but got no answer. Either they couldn't hear me, or they were hurt or dead. *No, no—Skye, stop it! Stop thinking like that.* I needed to find a way back up, and then I could figure out what had happened to the others.

It also frightened me that the Bahlari might be lurking around down here. I prayed the explosion had sidetracked them long enough for me to escape. At least I still had my pack. I knelt and reached around inside.

I counted ten granola bars, two bags of M&M's, and six water bottles. At least I wouldn't starve. My hand brushed something round at the bottom of the bag. I pulled out a slim cylinder and ran my fingers over it. A flashlight! I didn't remember putting it in there.

I found the switch with my thumb, praying that the batteries weren't dead. "Please let it work." I took a deep breath and pushed the button.

A flash of light sprang from the bulb. I wept. "Thank God."

Shining the light around the cavern made the room's corners seem darker and more ominous. Nothing moved. There was no sound except the whistle of the humid wind blowing up from below. I felt a sudden chill and hugged myself, feeling desperately alone and abandoned.

I tried not to panic. It might alert the Bahlari.

Fearful that the Bahlari were waiting for me somewhere inside this hideous pit, I sat frozen. Even though I had the flashlight, the darkness made me uneasy. Soft scurrying noises that made me think of rats raised the hairs on the back of my neck. I slowly moved the beam around, pointing it into the shadows.

I didn't know where I needed to go, but I knew I couldn't stay in the open, exposed in the middle of the pit. So I shined the light around into the cave's recesses, looking for a place to hide. I didn't want to go too far into the tunnels in case Paul and Nana came looking for me.

A group of boulders sitting against one of the walls looked like they offered some protection. I carried my pack over, sat down between the boulders, and leaned my head back.

The humid, warm air soothed me, and the cavern was silent. I was tired and used up. Tomorrow . . . maybe tomorrow . . . Paul and Nana will find me tomorrow. I clicked off the flashlight to save the batteries and closed my eyes. Just for a minute, I'll only rest a moment . . .

The sun is shining on our house in Phoenix, right across the street. Dad, wearing his fishing hat and shorts, is standing on the porch waving at me to come over. Mom comes out of the house in her fancy yellow sundress and stands beside Dad. They hold hands like they used to when I was a little girl.

"Skye, come home!" Mom calls to me, smiling. "We're waiting for you."

I run across the street into their arms. Dad hugs me tight while Mom rubs my back. "I love you," I say. "I love you both so much and miss you."

Mom pulls me into her arms. "I'm so sorry, Skye. So sorry. I was selfish. So sorry I left you alone."

"It's all right," I whisper. "It doesn't matter anymore. At least we're all together again . . ."

I sat bolt upright.

How long had I been out?

The cold slipped through my clothes, making my stiff joints ache even more. I turned on the flashlight and trembled, seeing a quick movement in front of me. I pointed the beam of light at it, and the flesh tensed across the back of my neck. Then, something moved on the opposite side of the pit. Dread hit my stomach like a punch.

A creepy noise was coming out of the dark tunnel. It reminded me of the time I spilled a box of cereal on the floor when I was a kid. The crisp crunch, crunch, crunch on the bottom of my feet as I rushed to clean up the mess.

Suddenly, a glowing cloud floated out of the tunnel shaft and headed my way. It was full of insect-like creatures. Forked lightning ignited and flickered through the cloud, illuminating countless legs and antennae of the creepy bugs inside.

Trapped, I backed against the cavern wall. The hideous cloud hovered over my face. I threw up my hands and screamed. The horrible insects started to attack my hair. I raised my hands to brush them away, but the cloud was like a sticky cobweb that stuck to my hands and skin.

The crisp crunching sound came in waves of clicks and snaps, getting louder and louder. I tried to squash the sickening insects between my fingers, but there were just too many. The creatures poked and jabbed at my closed eyes and mouth, trying to crawl inside my body. Unable to scream any longer, I gagged and coughed from the suffocating swarm of bugs.

I could feel one trying to pry my eye open with its cricket-like legs. I snatched it away from my cheek, and the sharp points on the legs drew blood. The blood on my face and hands drove the insects into a frenzy. I slashed at the swarm with my flashlight.

Hundreds crowded around me like a host of angry bees. The noise turned into an even louder buzzing and popping. I clenched my teeth to keep the insects out of my mouth. They buzzed in my ears, and I dropped to my knees to try and keep them away from my face.

No longer able to scream, breathe, or suffer any more torture, I rolled onto my stomach and curled into a fetal position. My mind had reached its ability to process the horror happening to me. I left my body and passed out.

I came to in the dark, lying on the cold hard ground, not knowing how I got there. The last few days were a blur in my mind. Tears clouded my eyes and ran down my cheek. My mind whirled with bits of memory: Dad running across the beach and jumping into the surf to join me in the water; consoling Mom at his funeral; cursing Mom for her addiction; the fight with Mom the night before she died; finding Paul's conch shell in the tide.

The shell.

The bugs.

I slapped at my eyes, tore through my hair, and shoved my hands inside my shirt, feeling for traces of insects. Nothing—nothing at all. Feeling around in the dark, my hand grasped the familiar cylinder of the flashlight. A beam of light flashed on, and I waved it around the chamber, looking for the swarm.

Nothing. The cavern was empty.

I blinked, a tear ran down my cheek, and I tasted the salty wetness on my tongue. Was I hallucinating? Had it really happened? I pointed the flashlight at the ground. There and there. Scattered across the cavern floor were squashed bodies and legs.

It was real. *Oh, God, it was real!*

A sickening feeling enveloped me. I panicked, shining the beam up and down the walls and on the ceiling, looking for more bugs. Nothing. They must have receded back into one of the tunnels. I'd rather die than try and survive another attack by that cloud again. I couldn't do it—wouldn't do it. No!

I stood up. "Paul, Nana, where are you?" I screamed.

I screamed and screamed until I wore myself out. Finally, I sat down on the floor, panting, and started to sob. I don't remember how long I carried on, but when I was done, I lifted my head, dried my eyes, and vowed that I was done with my pity party. I had to find a way out.

I rolled the cold cylinder between my palms. At least I had light. My backpack had stayed with me through the entire nightmare. At least I had food and water. I stood and stretched. I started ticking off all the positive things I had going for me: One–I wasn't injured. Two–I could walk. By the time I'd reached ten, I had finally calmed down.

Even though I didn't know what had happened to Nana and Paul, and I didn't know how I would find them, at least I had the means to get there. The horror of the attack lingered, but that had happened to a weaker girl. I was stronger than that now. I was ready to go on; no matter what happened, all I could do was die.

CHAPTER 29

DOUBTS

ʕ

I returned to where I had last seen Paul looking down from the cracked dome. The ledge above was silent and dark. I wondered if I could somehow climb back up the vertical slide that had brought me down here. But from where I stood, the smooth surface had no hand or footholds for climbing back up.

"Paul! Nana! Can anyone hear me?" I yelled as loud as I could. I stood and listened for an answer, then repeated my calls several times. Again, no response.

I stood inside my cocoon of light, surrounded by darkness, feeling trapped. Then my foot slipped, and I went down on my butt. I sat there, tears stinging my eyes. What was the use of getting up? There was nowhere to go. I might as well let the Bahlari get me.

"What's the use?" I whispered.

Closing my eyes, I took a deep breath and counted to ten.

"Now, get off your ass and pull yourself together."

I shrugged the pack off my shoulders and reached inside. I pulled out a towel and a pair of socks. First, I wrapped the towel around my head to shield my face; then, I put a sock over each hand like mittens. Satisfied, I took a swig from a water bottle. If those insects returned, I'd be ready.

I trudged back through the cavern with the narrow beam of light leading my way. My newfound bravery didn't keep me from looking over my shoulder every few moments, afraid that something awful was coming up from behind.

Where were Paul and Nana? Even though I was worried about calling attention to myself, I shouted out to them as I passed through the cave's dark passages. Soon, hopelessly lost, I went on out of instinct. I didn't know where I was going, but I had no choice. From then on, I had to be careful. The Bahlari could be lurking anywhere. This pit was hell, and hell had broken through to the surface of the Earth.

As I walked through the dark cave, I felt I was being watched. The feeling that something was lurking in the shadows haunted my mind.

I don't know how long I'd been walking, but my legs started to cramp. The effort of sidestepping rocks and boulders was exhausting.

I dropped my pack from my sore shoulders, dug out a water bottle, and tilted it to my lips, drinking half of it down in one swig. Then, pulling the bottle from my mouth, I realized I had to ration what was left. My gut tightened as I thought of being trapped down here in the dark without food or water.

Hunger replaced thirst, and I took a granola bar from the pack. I broke off a small piece and bit into it, wondering how long I could make the food last. Three days? Five days? A week?

"Stop it, Skye!" I told myself. There was no sense making myself panic. I had to take it one day at a time. Maybe if I ran out of food, I'd coax those bugs back and eat them. Plenty of people eat insects. They even have recipe books for them. Right then, I decided to do whatever it took to survive.

I shivered and rose from my place against the rock wall. I turned the flashlight on, worrying about conserving the batteries. Yet I couldn't even think of the batteries dying, not here, not alone in this dark cave—one thing at a time. But, on the other hand, if I ran out of food, water, or light, it didn't matter. I was dead anyway.

"Stop it, Skye," I scolded myself again. "Just move on and look for a way out. That's all that matters at this moment."

Never had I been so exposed and uncomfortable as in this damp, dark pit. At home in Phoenix, the sun always shined. Had I been dropped into this scenario back then, I would have probably curled up and died, unable to handle the terror I'd just gone through.

Movement on my right caused me to back against the wall and point the beam in that direction. I whimpered and strained my eyes, searching for shapes and outlines in the shadows. I couldn't afford to slip up and get myself killed with something lurking out there.

A burst of light from far off caused me to turn to the left. Then, to the right, the slight movement of a shadow caused me to twist in that direction and point the flashlight. A tall figure in a billowing black robe with bone-white claws hanging out of its sleeves stood in the beam. Its face was buried in the cloak's hood, but the thought of seeing it made me shudder.

Another flash of light to my left made me turn again. Black outlines of several other figures in robes drifted toward me. On my right, the other figure still loomed. These tall figures must be the Bahlari. I was surrounded. With no weapons to defend myself, I was going to die.

I backed away as they got closer. I stumbled, tripped on an outcropping rock, and fell to my knees. The Bahlari paced themselves, not in a hurry. Trembling, I stood, feeling like I was going mad. Tears rolled down my cheeks. I sobbed with terror but refused to scream. Instead, I scanned the cavern and shadows past the Bahlari, looking for a way to escape. The second's ticked by. The Bahlari were gathering, getting closer, and my options for escape were disappearing.

Then, with no warning, a hooded figure from the crowd soared forward. My head jerked up, and my fight-and-flight response kicked in. I rushed headlong toward the thing and brushed past its outreaching claws. I fled into the dark recesses of the cave toward the place I'd last seen the flashing lights.

Behind me, I heard the piercing shriek of the creature that almost had me in its clutches. I ran as fast as my long legs would carry me. The other Bahlari joined in. Screech after screech became a chorus of cries that echoed through the caverns.

The blood-curdling cries pushed me along, faster and faster, into a side tunnel where I'd seen the lights. My only thought was escaping the Bahlari and not being captured or killed. I kept this in my mind as my legs pumped into overtime as I rushed to meet my fate.

The thin beam of the flashlight kept me going forward, but I couldn't see rocks and debris in my path. I stumbled and fell, tearing my jacket again and ripping my pants. I picked myself up, gasping for air, wiped the blood off my palms, and stumbled blindly through the tunnel.

I heard footsteps behind me, turned my head to look, tripped over something big, and went down on my face. Picking myself up again, I flashed the light on what I had tripped over—a dead body in a tattered old uniform and leather flight jacket.

The head was missing.

"Oh, God," I croaked.

The flashlight beam reflected off something shiny around the corpse's waist. Gagging, I bent down for a closer look and saw the gleaming tip of a knife blade sticking out of a leather sheath.

I fiddled with the knife until it came free from the sheath. Standing up, I backed away from the sickening stench of the headless corpse. I slid the knife into the pocket of my jeans. Were the Bahlari trying to scare me with this mangled body so they could feed on my fear? Silently, I backed away. I tripped over a round rock and sent it sailing toward the body. The rolling object caught in the beam of my flashlight, and I stifled a shriek.

The severed head of the corpse came to rest next to the body. Then, as the flashlight's beam swung in my hand, hundreds of roaches blew out of the skull and scurried across the ground at my feet.

I staggered back, retching, and fell to the ground. The bile rose in my throat as I felt crawling roaches on my arms and legs. I leaped up and danced around, swatting the nasty things from my body as I ran as fast as possible to escape the horror in front of me.

Suddenly, I stopped in my tracks. The beam of light shined dark ahead of me—the cliff's edge. I pointed the flashlight over the side into total darkness. I sank onto the ledge, trembling, stiff, sore, exhausted, and miserable, looking over the precipitous drop. A roach ran out of the collar of my jacket and over my cheek. I grabbed it and flung it over the edge.

Just what I needed, another hurdle to cross.

CHAPTER 30

BETRAYAL

My head ached from dodging the Bahlari, all those awful bugs, and the headless dead soldier. Leaning over the rim of the ledge, I shined the beam against the rock wall that supported the shelf I was sitting on. It was riddled with volcanic-type holes that looked like Swiss cheese. Maybe I could use the cavities as footholds to climb down.

With the flashlight off, I strained hard to hear something against the silence of the cave. The only sound was my breathing echoing off the walls. I listened as hard as possible but heard nothing coming from behind me. That didn't mean that the Bahlari weren't still out there. Maybe they'd sunk back into the bowels of hell.

I was kidding myself. The Bahlari weren't going to leave me alone. They were playing a game with me. My fear provided them with food. They would continue to taunt me with unspeakable horrors until they drove me out of my mind. I felt sick, so I squeezed my eyes shut to keep from throwing up or passing out. I dropped the backpack from my shoulders. My aching muscles strained as I reached over to unzip the pack. I rummaged around inside as silently as possible, feeling for a water bottle.

Twisting it open, I tossed it to my lips, chugging down a few swallows. I wanted more, but I stopped. It was important to ration everything I had left.

My stomach gurgled and rumbled, telling me I was hungry. Quietly, I reached inside the pack and felt around for an energy bar. Tearing through the wrapper, I ripped into the bar with my teeth. I couldn't remember tasting anything more delicious in my life. My jaw slowed, savoring every morsel of the bar. My common sense said I should save part of it, but I needed the energy to find Nana and Paul.

Picking up my pack, I threw it over my shoulders and snapped on the flashlight. I clenched my teeth and took a deep breath, ready to go back and face the horrors I had just left. It was either that or climb down the steep wall into the bowels of hell.

My breathing sped up as, once again, I hiked back to where I'd last seen Paul. The picture I formed in my mind of that hideous headless corpse and the roaches shifted back and forth in my brain. Then, to keep from screaming, I painted a picture in my mind of happier times at the beach with Mom and Dad.

The beam traced the outline of the head lying on the ground. There was no sign of the roaches, so I ran the light around the skull for a closer examination. The skin was leather-like, and the eye sockets were empty. I wondered who this poor soul was and what he was doing in this dark tomb.

Was this going to be my fate? Dying alone in the roach-infested darkness?

A dark figure hovered in the shadows to my left. I jerked away from the sinister form and threw myself against the rock wall of the cavern. I stood still, listening, my heart pounding. Whatever was there was coming for me and getting closer. I couldn't make out its shape, but the enormous thing was coming fast now. In a few seconds, it would be on me. I wanted to run, but my feet were rooted to the ground. My heart was jumping out of my chest.

As the faceless figure floated toward me, my hands flew up to my face, and I shrieked. The sound was shrill inside the cave. I knew that scream would bring more Bahlari, but I couldn't help myself.

An arm extended from the robe of the hooded figure, and its clawed hand reached out for me. Jagged pointed teeth grew from behind lips that appeared when it opened its mouth.

Cringing at the revolting creature, I stood pressed against the wall with nowhere to go. Then, the sound of more Bahlari approaching from the back of the cave kicked me into gear. I willed my legs to move and ran past the outstretched claw into the darkness.

If only there had been light in the cave, it would have made me feel less vulnerable. But unfortunately, it was impossible to see what lurked in the shadows outside the narrow beam. There was nothing else I could do; I stumbled back toward the ledge where I had just been.

When I reached the overhang, I shined the beam down onto the holes in the rock wall. I could hear the rustling of those things coming closer. I turned off the flashlight and pulled my legs over the precipice, moving as quietly as possible so as not to attract the Bahlari's attention.

I took a deep breath and slowly felt my way along the holes in the wall where the handgrips and footholds were. I scooted down the rock like a spider. I had no idea how far down the ground was, so I took it one moment at a time—one foot, the next, one-hand grip, and the next. On and on, slowly working my way down.

Sweat beaded my forehead, but I didn't wipe it away, fearing it would make my hand slippery. My hands were stinging; I had already slipped a few times and hurt my foot by kicking out at the rock wall to break my fall. The angle got steeper with every step I descended. It felt like I was hanging against this wall for hours, but it was probably less. The terror of climbing down in the dark made the time stretch out. My arms and legs were sore and numb from the exertion.

My foot missed a foothold. I stumbled and threw my hands out to catch myself but missed and slid down the cliff face. The sound of my scream startled me as I landed in a crunch at the foot of the wall.

I couldn't have fallen far, or I would have died. I stretched my body out and checked for broken bones. Everything worked, so I brushed myself off and stood listening for some reaction to my scream.

No sound, nothing. Only dark, stale air. Trying to make as little noise as possible, I rummaged inside my jacket pocket for the flashlight. I grimaced as I hit the button. The beam flashed on, and I checked out my surroundings. The cavern floor flattened out to a series of tunnels that twisted off into the sides of the walls.

A banging noise echoed inside one of the tunnels, and the hair stood up on the back of my neck. I froze, doused the beam, and listened: only silence. Maybe I'd imagined the sound. But, no, it started up again. This time, it was footsteps from inside the tunnel. Again, I stood frozen, waiting for the steps to fade. Instead, they got louder and closer.

I tiptoed to one of the other side tunnels, slid inside, pressed myself against the wall, and listened. Everything was quiet. Afraid to turn on my light, I moved down the dark tunnel by feeling along the rock wall. I came to a fork where the tunnel split and, seeing a dim light off in the distance to the right, decided to go toward it. I didn't know whether to be afraid, but I decided to follow the light. The alternative was to remain cowering in the dark tunnels waiting for something to attack me. At least I had the upper hand by sneaking up on whoever owned the light.

The glowing light was flickering, not constant. As I got closer, the smell of candle wax filled the air. The tunnel was bathed in a soft glow from giant ancient wax pots recessed in the wall. I stood and listened for sound in the passageway. Off in the distance, I could hear faint sobs. It didn't sound dangerous; it sounded like someone was in trouble.

As I ran down the corridor, the sobbing got louder. It was Nana! My feet carried me farther down the tunnel, and I came to a thick old wooden door on the side of the rock wall. It seemed strange that the door was bolted from the outside. A small window with metal bars had been notched out in the wood. I stood on my tiptoes and looked through the bars.

Nana was sitting against the wall on the bare ground, moaning. I backed up, lifted the heavy bolt on the door, and threw it open. I ran inside, leaned down, and kissed her cheek.

"Skye! You're alive!" Nana cried out. She threw her arms around me. Her voice echoed through the cell.

I pulled back to look into her eyes. "Did someone hurt you?"

Nana shook her head. "No, honey. I was upset because I thought you were dead."

"Where's Paul?"

"I don't know. We were separated when they captured us."

I reached out and touched her sweet face and pushed the soft silver hair away from her eyes. Then, I stood and reached out to help pull Nana up. "Let's get out of here."

Behind me, a hand touched my shoulder. Startled, I twisted around. Kitori's solemn face looked down at me.

"Did you lock Nana up? And where's Paul?" I hissed.

"We've taken care of him." Kitori squared his shoulders and reached out to take my hand. "Come with me."

"Not until you tell me what's going on." I snapped my hand back, lashed out, and slapped his treacherous face.

CHAPTER 31

SEEING STARS

Kitori rubbed his cheek, and we stared at each other in silence. How long had he been involved with the Bahlari? And what about Tansy? Was she a traitor too?

"Did you hear what I said? Get your ass moving!" Kitori reached out to grab my arm, but I smacked it away.

"Don't touch me!" I spat.

Kitori smiled, a slick, sinister sneer. "Do you want to know about your mama? She's rotting in Hell for killing herself. It's your fault, you know? You drove her to suicide. All you cared about was dear old daddy. You could have cared less about her. In fact, you wished her dead!"

Nana stood straight up. "Shut your filthy mouth! You don't know anything about our family."

I turned to Nana. "It's OK. We're leaving. He can't hurt me with his lies." My outstretched hand gripped Nana's, and we marched past Kitori for the door.

"You're not going anywhere!" Kitori reached out and wrapped his arms around my chest.

I reared back and slammed him in the shin with my heel. Nana whacked him in the head with her backpack. She pulled back for another hit, but Kitori grabbed the strap and took the pack.

"Give that back! It belongs to me!" Nana screamed.

"It used to belong to you," Kitori smirked.

"Give it back to her!" I yelled.

"Shut up," Kitori snapped.

Nana stepped forward with her hand out. "I want my pack, and I want it now. If you're going to kill me, you better do it. Either give me back my bag, or I'm taking it from you."

Kitori held the pack out, the strap balanced on his index finger, and grinned. He was taunting her, daring her to come and get it.

"That's it!" Nana rushed over to grab the pack, but Kitori lifted it over his head out of her reach. I reared back and kicked him in the knee.

Kitori let out a screech, and Nana grabbed the pack.

"Let's go!" I grabbed Nana's hand and ran for the door. Kitori was right behind us. As soon as we cleared the door, I turned and slammed it in Kitori's face. Then, I threw the outside bolt, locking Kitori in the cell.

I turned to Nana. "Why did you fight Kitori for the pack?"

"That son of a bitch is strong." Nana held up the pack. "The shell was stuffed in the bottom. I couldn't let him have it. We might need it, if only for light."

Kitori's muffled screams echoed from behind the door. "You can't get away. I'll find you bitches! You'll be sorry!"

"Stuff it, Kitori!" Nana held up her middle finger and coughed. "My gosh darned throat is on fire."

I slid the straps off my shoulders, dug around in my pack, and held out a water bottle. "At least he didn't take my pack either. I still have the flashlight, water, and some food."

Nana reached over and took the water.

"What happened after we got separated?" I asked.

"I was trapped on the dome platform with Paul after the collapse sent you to the bottom. I kept screaming your name, but you didn't answer. Paul told me to be quiet because the Bahlari might hear and come for us. But I didn't stop," Nana said. "I thought you might be hurt. Right after that, Kitori found us."

"But why were you locked in the cell?"

"According to Kitori, it was for my protection against the Bahlari."

"Did you believe him?"

"I didn't know what to believe. Kitori told Paul he would help him search for you and that I would be safe in the cell. Kitori appears to be immune to the Bahlari. He certainly isn't afraid of them. I didn't want to face a group of those horrible creatures, so I did what he said."

Something was bothering me. Something was missing—something key that would make sense out of this madness. "It just seems weird that the Bahlari wouldn't attack him," I said. "Either they are allies, or something else keeps the Bahlari from killing him. Do you have any ideas?"

"Maybe the Bahlari have taken over his mind?" Nana said. "I'm not sure."

We walked hand in hand down the tunnel corridor. It soon turned to total darkness. I slipped my pack off and fished for the flashlight. When I turned it on, the beam flickered and died.

"Oh, no." I shook the flashlight, hoping there was a bad connection with the batteries, but it didn't come back on.

"Nana, grab the wall," I said. "We'll have to feel our way down the tunnel."

"The hell with that," she said. "There's no way to tell if the Bahlari are lurking around. I have the shell. Remember?"

Nana pulled out the shell. The light it emanated lit up the corridor. Then, a scraping noise that sounded like a bunch of puppies' paws running across a slippery wood floor came out of the darkness not far behind us.

"Nana, we better hurry; something's coming."

We took off running, but Nana stumbled and fell. I went back to where she lay. She handed me the shell, and I helped her to her feet. But it was too late. The strange noise was gaining on us. There was no escape.

A whoosh of air blew past me. A claw extended out of the sleeve of a robe, about to touch my face. I cringed backward, and a talon glided past my cheek like a snake. I turned my head, afraid to look at the thing, but curiosity told me I must. Forcing my head around, I stared into the face of evil, crocodile-like eyes, green with oval slits, wide nostrils, and fangs growing out of a mouth like a blood-sucking leech.

"Get away from her!" Nana screamed.

The Bahlari turned toward Nana. It was so fast, so sudden, I thought I was hallucinating. It raised its claws threateningly at Nana, and I raised the shell to strike it in the head. It backed off and raced down the dark tunnel. Its cold presence lingered, and I shivered.

We took off running down the tunnel as fast as we could go. Nana was having difficulty keeping up, so I took her hand and pulled her along. The tunnel opened into an enormous cavern, and we ran right into a pack of Bahlari waiting for us.

"Let's turn around and go back," I yelled.

We ran back into the tunnel and only got about twenty feet before we ran into Kitori, leading another group of Bahlari in our direction.

"We're trapped!" I cried.

We did an about-face and made a mad dash back to the cavern. Where were we going to run—where were we going to hide? My body trembled, and my bones ached. I wanted to stop running. But I was no longer that weak, vulnerable girl from Phoenix. I was stronger now.

When we reached the cavern, a group of Bahlari blocked our entrance. Behind us, Kitori and his minions were almost on us. We were trapped hundreds of feet below the Grand Canyon in a dark tunnel. No one knew we were here. If they killed us, we could end up like the headless soldier—insect food.

Nana turned and faced Kitori. "Let's quit screwing around. You've got us trapped. If you're going to kill me, do it now, but let Skye go. She never did anything to deserve to die. Otherwise, tell us what you want?"

Kitori stood motionless, challenging her with a glare. Then, his gaze shifted from Nana to me. He raised a hand and pointed at the shell I was holding. "I want the shell," he said.

"No!" I wrapped my arms tight around the shell.

"Either you give me the shell, or I'll take it from you," Kitori sneered.

"Don't take the shell," Nana pleaded. "Please don't. Take me. Let Skye go."

"What would we want with you, old woman?" Kitori snickered.

I stepped forward, suddenly angry, "Stop it!" I cried. "Nana, come over to me."

Nana inched closer. I reached out and grabbed her hand, pulling her against me. My heart was pounding as I lifted the shell over my head in defiance. "You're not getting the shell! I'll smash it to bits before I let you lay your filthy hands on it."

Kitori tensed. His eyes hardened as he backed up a few steps. "Don't be foolish. If you destroy the shell, you have nothing left to bargain with. It will sign your death warrant."

"Don't come any closer," I warned, with the shell clutched in my hand. I was ready to slam it to the ground.

Kitori studied my face for any sign of weakness. Sweat gathered on my forehead and under my arms, but I held my ground. I was playing poker with the devil, and the stakes were high.

The Bahlari hung back, watching the show. Then, several more figures appeared behind the group from the cavern's rear. As they pushed their way through to the front, I could see they had Paul. He was struggling, held parallel to the ground in the grip of their mighty arms and claws.

"Paul!" I stumbled, almost dropping the shell.

Paul's blue eyes peered out at me through his battered face. I sensed his pain. Not just from his wounds, but his failure to keep us safe.

The Bahlari dragged his body across the ground and dropped it at Kitori's feet. Kitori kicked out with his foot and busted Paul's lip. His head bounced off the ground, and blood squirted down his chin, staining his torn shirt.

"This is just the beginning," Kitori said, glaring into my face. "I'll kill him unless you give me that shell."

Paul rolled onto his back and kicked out at Kitori, knocking him to the ground. "Do not give him the shell, Skye," Paul grunted.

Kitori recovered and pulled himself up. He came around and kicked Paul in the head with his boot. Paul's head reared back, and blood splattered across the cave floor. His clear blue eyes shone through the crimson fluid covering his face.

I couldn't stand Paul being tortured any longer. "Here," I held out the shell. "Take it! It's not worth a shit to me! Just don't hurt Paul anymore!"

Kitori came forward with a smirk on his face, and his hand flew out to take the shell.

My hand reached out to Kitori, but I tossed the shell down to Paul.

Kitori blinked, trying to fathom what just happened, and lowered his hand.

Paul stood up and held the shell over his head. Stars poured from the shell, cascading down his body, washing the blood from his face and healing his wounds. The points of light rose and grew and covered the cave's walls and ceiling.

There was light. Brilliant, blinding light, glowing like a thousand stars, a million stars. They danced and shimmered around the cavern. The light reflected off my eyes, my hair, and my body. The light lit up Nana's wide eyes and reflected off the cave's walls, making it seem like we were standing in sunlight.

The stars flared like diamonds, and light sizzled in threads of platinum. They followed a pattern like a chain reaction with bursts of light that flared and fizzled and burst again in a hypnotic sequence.

The Bahlari scattered, running into each other in their haste to escape. One of the creatures sailed past me, and I could see the agony that the stars of light caused it. Its lizard's eyes cinched shut as it howled in pain from being pelted by the stars that burnt its skin like fire.

"Look, Nana!" I pointed at the Bahlari running through the cavern, trying to brush off the points of light attacking them from every angle.

Nana smiled. "Thank God for Alien Paul. He saved our asses again."

CHAPTER 32

AFTERSHOCK

Nana and I stood by and watched Paul shoot down the Bahlari with the stars from the shell. It burned them. Their howls and shrieks echoed throughout the cavern. No matter how fast they tried to escape, the stars circled the cave until they flushed them out and charred them.

Nana raised a fist in the air and shouted. "We're beating the crap out of them!"

Out of the corner of my eye, I saw a dark figure slithering up behind Nana.

"Nana, watch out!" I cried.

Nana saw the panic on my face and turned around. Kitori wielded a knife in his fist and raised it toward her face. Nana slapped his fist away with her hand, and the blade slashed across her palm. I ran to help Nana, but she threw a kick, and Kitori stumbled against the cave wall.

Kitori stood up and held up the knife. "That was a mistake. You bitches are dead. Starting with you." He pointed the blade at me and charged. I threw up my hands to protect my face. Nana put her foot out and tripped him before he could reach me. Kitori went flying and lay sprawled across the ground.

As he sat up, the look on his face was pure evil.

"Nana, run!" I cried.

Before she could move, Kitori pulled his arm back and flung the knife at Nana.

She went down on her knees with the blade buried in her stomach. Dark red blood gushed out of the wound. I screamed and fell to my knees beside her. I pressed my hands over the wound, but it wouldn't stop bleeding. The blood poured over my hands, staining them red. All the blood was Nana's, and I couldn't stop it.

"Paul!" I screamed, "Paul! Help us!"

Kitori ran off through one of the side tunnels.

Continuing to hold the shell above his head, Paul was unaware of what had happened. He lowered the shell and looked my way.

"Kitori stabbed Nana!" I shouted.

I looked down at Nana. Her eyes were weak, and a line of more blood ran from her lips and down her chin.

"Oh, Nana," I sighed, fighting back the tears.

"I'm OK." Nana coughed up blood.

She was not OK.

Paul kneeled beside us on the ground. "Do something. Help her," I begged him.

He reached out his hand and worked it under mine, applying pressure. I held out my bloody palms and wiped them on my jeans, waiting for his hands to glow and mend her wound like he'd done with her eye.

The seconds turned into minutes, and nothing happened. Instead, Nana coughed up more blood.

"Paul? What's wrong? Your magic touch isn't working!" I was panicking.

"The shell must have zapped my power," Paul said.

"Paul! You have to do something!" I cried. "There's so much blood!"

Nana raised her head and looked at her bleeding stomach. "I've made a mess. Don't ask me where it hurts," she said.

"Lie still. You're going to be OK, Nana." I burst into tears.

Nana wiped the blood from her lips. "That's a stupid thing to say. Of course, I'm not going to be OK," she panted. "Just get me out of here."

The sound of thunder rushing down the tunnel made us turn our heads. An ATV flew out of the corridor and entered the cavern, coming to a screeching halt. The driver jumped out.

"Tansy!" I cried.

"Hurry, get inside," she said.

"Nana's hurt. Do you know a way out?" I asked.

Paul was bent over Nana, trying to suppress the bleeding. He looked up at Tansy. "How do I know we can trust you? Kitori tried to kill Nana."

"Kitori fell under the influence of the Bahlari. They brainwashed him. I escaped before they could capture me, too," Tansy said. "Where's he now?"

"He ran off after he stabbed Nana. We better get Nana out of here. She needs medical help," I urged Tansy.

"We need to get you into the vehicle," Paul told Nana. "Can you stand if I help you up?"

"I don't know," Nana said. "But I'll try."

I went over to help Paul with Nana. "I'll get her arm if you can carry most of her weight," I said.

We pulled Nana up, and she collapsed into Paul's arms. We laid her back on the ground.

"I'll take her feet, and you can get her arms," Tansy said. "Then, we can carry her to the ATV and set her in the front seat."

"She will have to sit in the back," Paul said. "One of us has to control the bleeding with pressure."

"Let's go. We're wasting time," I pleaded.

Tansy grabbed Nana's feet, and Paul took her shoulders while I held my hands against her wound. We carried her over to the vehicle and helped her into the backseat. I climbed in next to her, and Paul buckled her harness and mine.

Tansy started the vehicle. It roared to life, and we took off down the same tunnel she'd driven through. Nana slumped against the restraints, barely conscious. Her breathing was labored.

I pushed my bloody hands against the wound. The pain in Nana's face was horrible to look at; her eyelids fluttered as she clung to my arm. I knew she was dying and probably wouldn't make it out of the cave in time to get help. "Hold on, Nana," I cried.

"Can't we go any faster?" I yelled to Tansy over the roar of the engine.

"I'm going as fast as I dare. I don't want to roll this thing and kill us all," Tansy screamed back.

"Pull over!" Paul yelled. "I will drive."

"That's crazy. You don't know where to go," Tansy answered.

"You can direct me. My reflexes will allow me to go much faster than you can safely drive," Paul shouted to her.

Tansy slammed on the brakes. In a moment, they changed places. Paul stood on the gas, and we jerked forward and accelerated at an alarming pace. The headlights and off-road light bar reflected off the coarse rock walls of the tunnel but couldn't penetrate the dark fifty feet ahead.

"When we come to a fork in the tunnel, veer right and keep going for a few more miles," Tansy yelled. "Then the tunnel opens into a cavern that leads to an ancient volcanic chute that will take us back to the surface."

Paul looked at Tansy and nodded.

"When we start the climb, be sure to keep up the speed on the vehicle, or we could roll back into the cavern or crash off the side into the abyss," Tansy shouted.

We sped through the tunnel and came out the cavern entering the chute. Inertia pushed my body against the seat. I closed my eyes as we began the vertical ascent to the surface. The high-pitched whine of the screaming engine made me open them. I swore I was on one of those scary roller coaster rides at Six Flags Magic Mountain. I tried to look at Nana, but we were going so fast I was glued against the seat, unable to move my head.

The ATV flew out of the volcanic crater onto a flat rock field on a shelf above the river. It came skidding to a stop ten feet from plunging over the cliff into the mighty Colorado. Paul jumped out of the driver's seat and leaned over the backseat to check on Nana.

"Oh, God," Nana whispered through the blood caked on her lips.

"Paul!" I screamed. "Let's go! We're wasting time. We need to get Nana to a hospital."

Nana's bloody hand reached up and brushed my arm. "No hospital. It's too late for that." She coughed, and blood poured out of her mouth.

"Oh, Nana." Tears rolled down my cheek. "You're going to be all right."

Clouds hung low over the canyon, and the sun peered out.

"Do you see it?" Nana's index finger pointed to the sky.

"See what?" I asked.

"The sun. It warms my face. I haven't seen the sun in for oh . . . so long. It feels good."

"We better get going," I said to Paul.

"No, wait," Nana coughed. "Just wait."

"Are you in pain?" I asked her.

"Just help me get out of this gadget. I want to lay on the ground and feel the sun."

"I looked at Paul. "We can't take her out. She will die."

"I won't make it out of here anyway," Nana said. "Get me on the ground and let me go in peace."

"Oh, no," I pleaded with Paul. "We can't!"

"We must fulfill her wishes," Paul answered.

Paul reached in and released Nana's harness. Her body slumped to my side, and a sob escaped my lips. By the time he leaned over and released my harness, I had decided to do as Nana wished.

Paul reached over to cover Nana's wound with a bandana wrapped around his hand while I climbed out of the backseat and stood in the sun with the breeze blowing across my cheeks.

I pulled the fleece throw from my pack and spread it across a patch of brittle grass in the sun. Paul put his arms around Nana, lifted her out of the vehicle, and gently laid her on the blanket. He kneeled at her side with his hand pressed against her wound.

Smiling, Nana lifted her head toward the sky. "Oh, God. The sun. So beautiful." Tears sprang from her eyes.

Nana turned her head to me and lifted her hand. I grasped it and knelt beside her. We looked into each other's tear-stained eyes, and I kissed the back of her hand.

"I'm proud of you, Skye. You have grown into quite a strong young woman."

"Don't leave me, Nana," I cried.

"It's all right. Let me go. You and I are headed in different directions now." Nana looked over at Paul but spoke to me. "Do you love him?"

"Yes," I answered.

Nana's fingers squeezed mine. "He's a good man . . . alien . . . whatever. Hold on to him. Take care of each other. I wish I could be there for you. But it looks like it's not meant to be."

"Oh, Nana, please hold on," I cried.

"The sun feels good." Nana's hand slid from mine, and she laid it on her chest. "I'm tired now. I want to sleep." Nana closed her eyes and drew her last breath.

Paul reached out his hand. I grasped it, and he pulled me to him and put his arms around me. I drew a deep breath and inhaled his sweet scent. His face was blurred through my tears while I clung to him. The sun warmed our shoulders as we stood around Nana's lifeless body.

Tansy came over and joined us as I held onto Paul.

"We have to call 911 and have someone come and get Nana's body," I said.

"We cannot bring the authorities into this," Tansy said. "She was stabbed, and there will be a homicide investigation. That will bring the unwanted attention of the police and the media into the area."

"We can't just leave her here for the animals to eat," I cried. "How will I explain what happened to her when I get home?"

"We have a doctor in the village that will certify a death certificate for her. He will say that she died of natural causes," Tansy replied.

"But what about her body? We can't just leave her here."

Paul reached out and took my arm. "I have a solution to the problem. We cremate her body."

I pulled back from his touch. "How? We can't light her on fire."

"No, it would not be hot enough to reduce her to ashes. I can use the shell. You saw what it did to the Bahlari."

"No!" I cried. "You can't do that to Nana."

"It's the only way," Tansy said. "Otherwise, there will be repercussions that none of us can deal with, including legal ramifications."

"Tansy is right," Paul said. "We cannot afford to draw attention to us or this placc. Nana would have understood."

I didn't want to agree with them, but I couldn't come up with a better solution. "OK, let's do it," I said. "Nana is gone, and we have to do something with her body."

Paul carried the shell over to Nana's body. He held it out, and it glowed in his hands. The colored bands circled and vibrated faster and faster. Then, a flash of golden light shot out from inside the shell. The light covered Nana like a blanket. Her body pulsed and glowed; within moments, she crumbled into ash.

Nana's blue eye stared up at me from the ashes. "Oh, my God!" I turned away.

Paul swooped down, picked up Nana's eye, and dropped it in the shell.

"What are you doing? I asked.

"It is part of me that was part of her. It cannot be destroyed. I put it back where it belongs."

"Is Nana still in there?" I asked, referring to the eye. "Her consciousness, her soul?" I wanted to know, to believe, that part of Nana was still alive.

"Part of her essence, her soul, remains in the eye," Paul said.

"Is it possible that Nana can ever return?"

Paul walked over, reached out, and hugged me against his chest. "I do not know. She was an intelligent, complex human. If anyone can transcend death, it would be Nana."

I glanced down at the shell in his hand. "Then it's over," I squeezed Paul tight. "My family's gone, and I'm all alone."

"You are not alone." Paul leaned in and kissed me. "I will not leave you."

"What are we going to do?" I pulled away. "The Bahlari are still out there. Can we kill the rest of them with the shell?"

"One thing at a time," Paul said. "First, we need to care for Nana."

We quietly gathered up Nana's ashes. Paul and I dug a shallow grave with our hands in a clearing not shaded by trees. We put her ashes inside and covered them with dirt. We gathered rocks and made a cairn to mark her grave. I hugged the shell against my chest and recited a prayer over the spot where Nana rested in the sun.

We climbed into the ATV. Tansy was at the wheel, and we headed to her village to map out a plan for dealing with the remainder of the Bahlari. I sat in the backseat, clutching the shell in my lap. I would protect it and keep it with me for the rest of my life. I didn't know if part of Nana was still inside it or what other powers it possessed, but I was ready to start a new life with Paul.

I stared at the side of Paul's face in the front seat. I loved him and knew he loved me; that was half the battle. We had magic. We had the shell, and I was ready to face whatever came next.